TWO ROOMS

Two Rooms At The End Of The World

Through a mutual agreement, we got that aching feeling
To look up one another one more time
Tracking down the zip codes
Sealing down those envelopes
Lack of communication on the telephone line.

But don't judge us by distance
Or the differences between us
Try to look at it with an open mind
For where there is one room, you'll always find another
Two rooms, at the end of the world.

Well we've both ridden the wagon bit the tail off the dragon
Borne our swords like steel knights on the highway
Washing down the dirt roads
Hosing off our dirty clothes
Coming to terms with the times that we couldn't but we tried

Where there is one room, you'll always find another
Two rooms, at the end of the world.
Where there is one room, you'll always find another
Two rooms, at the end of the world.

Door to door they would whisper, will they ever get together
Their rooms are different temperatures I'm told
There's a change in their thinking
And their habits seem uneven
But together the two of them were mining gold

ELTON JOHN & BERNIE TAUPIN IN THEIR OWN WORDS

TWO ROOMS

ELTON JOHN & BERNIE TAUPIN

IN THEIR OWN WORDS

B⊕XTREE

This edition first published in the UK 1992
by BOXTREE LIMITED, Broadwall House,
21 Broadwall, London SE1 9PL
Hardback edition first published by
Boxtree Limited 1991

ISBN 1-85283-788-8

Art and design direction: Wherefore Art
Interviews compiled by: Lorna Dickinson &
                        Claudia Rosencrantz
Picture Editor: Kate Warde-Aldam
Editors: Simon Prytherch & Jonny Ffinch

Typeset by Cambrian Typesetters, Frimley, Surrey.
Printed in Italy by New Interlitho

A CIP catalogue record for this book is available from the
British Library

CONTENTS	PAGE

– *INTRODUCTION* –

Elton John and Bernie Taupin together
make one of the most successful songwriting partnerships in the history of
popular music.

Complementing the remarkable Tribute
Album, on which sixteen of the world's
top artists have recorded their
own versions of favourite songs, 'Two
Rooms' – the book, charts in Elton and
Bernie's own words the origin and develop-
ment of a career that has spanned 25 years
and over 200 compositions.

Friends and relatives have added their own
comments, shedding light on this unique
collaboration; a creative relationship that has
been both independent and interdependent –
Two Rooms at the end of the world.

Elton and Bernie 1989

Bernie aged 9

Elton aged 7

Bernie aged 2 with his parents

'My early influences were Jerry Lee Lewis and Little Richard, because they're by far and away the best Rock and Roll piano players'

Elton aged 4

Tell me about your childhood.

EJ I was born in fairly humble circumstances, in a sort of semi-detached council house in England. My father was in the Royal Air Force and because he was away so much of the time, I was really brought up by my grandmother and my auntie.

What were some of your early musical influences?

EJ I came from a musical family in as much that my father played the trumpet in a dance band and my auntie Win played the piano. There was a piano in my grandmother's house, and there were always records. My parents bought records; it was the 1950s, so it was mostly things like Coastline, Nat King Cole, Frankie Laine, Johnny Ray, Guy Mitchell, Joe Stafford and Rosemary Clooney. My father liked George Shearing, who's still one of the best pianists of all time in my opinion. And I played the piano at a very early age, I think I was three when I started to play by ear. When Rock 'n' Roll came into my life, I was obviously a much bigger fan of someone who played the piano, than someone who played the guitar. Later I got into Rhythm & Blues and Fats Domino. But my main influences, I would have to say, were Jerry Lee Lewis and Little Richard, because they're by far and away the best Rock 'n' Roll piano players.

BT I know in this day and age it's very unhip to admit that your childhood was great but I'd say in a word it was idyllic. I was blessed with really great parents, parents that never challenged me, never asked why I did what I did, they were always there backing me up. I was brought up on a farm, in a family that was transplanted from France and southern England to Lincolnshire; it was a

Bernie aged 2

blending of cultures. It wasn't the archetypal northern family tradition that I grew up in. I look back on it with great fondness. What I do now grew from that.

How did you discover poetry?

BT I discovered poetry through my grandfather on my mother's side and my mother as well. From an early age I remember them reading poetry to me which is strange because you'd think they would be reading me something else, even if it was the classics or just current books of the time. They read narrative poetry to me because it was something that they loved and when I heard it around me I gained a natural affinity for it. When I was a kid, I didn't play the games of the day. But I can remember playing things that were inspired by narrative poetry. My grandfather would read me things like *The Ancient Mariner* and *Lochinvar*, and I'd tear down the hills outside my house

wielding my wooden sword being Lochinvar, while all the other kids were going, "Lochin who?"

Would you describe yourself as a loner?

BT I was definitely a loner. I invented all my own entertainment. I spent a lot of time on my own. I only had one elder brother and we never spent any time together. I don't remember playing with him once. I remember getting into arguments and fighting. That's not to say we didn't care about each other, we both had different interests and different attitudes even as young children and that's remained the case up to this point. But that only lasted till I was in my early teens and then I found a series of friends. I had three close friends from the time I was about thirteen up to the time I went to London.

When did your interest in the American West start?

BT The American West entered from the first time I

watched television and listened to the radio. The first music that I listened to were people like Huddie Ledbetter, Woody Guthrie, Sonny Terry and Brownie McGee. And then I got into listening to people like Marty Robbins and Johnny Cash. There was an album of Marty Robbins called *Trail Songs and Gunfighter Ballads* which I must have worn out. One of the reasons I wanted to write songs was hearing Marty Robbins' *El Paso*. That's where a lot of the imagery in our songs has come from – the narrative poetry that I listened to, then the narrative songs of Marty Robbins and Johnny Cash and Johnnie Horton's *North to Alaska*, which

"Bernie was really interested in poetry, in books, and words. I have a passion for books and reading, so I hope I've passed that on to him. He used to know a lot of poetry by heart, and write very long epic poems. He was very interested in Americana, and he loved stories about the Alamo and he used to make models of battles of the civil war."

Bernie's Mum

were like epic poems. I mean had Tennyson had a piano, he probably would have written a melody to *The Charge of the Light Brigade*. That's where my affinity with the American West came from. Not from what John Ford conjured up in Westerns and not what TV conjured up with Hopalong Cassidy and the Lone Ranger because I never related to that. I always related to the reality of the West. And the reality of it was Woody Guthrie and Huddie Ledbetter; the mining camps and the dust bowl. I like the grittiness of that and the dirtiness of it. I couldn't get into the silver pistols and bullets and all that shit, it wasn't the

real thing and I think I've always gone for the real thing. I never liked to compromise, you've got to go straight for the heart.

When did you first start writing?

BT I started writing when I went to school at five years old. My favourite thing, even before I went to secondary school, was writing essays, even the old what-did-you-do-on-your-weekend. Unfortunately what I did on my weekend tended to get a little exaggerated, my imagination being what it is. One of my earliest literary experiences was when I was eleven or twelve – I decided I wanted to write a book. As I've said I was very into Americana and the American West, so I decided to write the history of the American West. I sat down to write it, and it was three pages long. I've always thought it was quite amusing; the history of the American West being three pages long, most of which I'd copied out of books anyway. I sent this grand tome, this enormous literary achievement, off to some publisher in London, and got a letter back saying: "Dear Mr. Taupin (I was eleven years old) there's nothing we can do with your book right now". But they said that I had some talent in the writing department and why didn't I try again a little later in life. And I thought that was great, the fact that they even wrote back to me. Noël Coward said until you've papered your room with rejection slips you're nobody. So at least I had one to start with.

Do you remember the first record you bought?

BT I think it was Lonnie Donnegan's *Rock Island Line*, before I realised that Huddie Ledbetter wrote it. I bought it as a 78 because I couldn't find it on a 45. Those were the days when record players used to play 78.

Elton aged 9

Can you remember the first single or the first music that really affected you?

EJ I've always liked all sorts of music, if it's well done, I can listen to it. I'm not that keen on really 'out there' jazz, and I'm not that keen on some classical music. Sitting through 45 minutes of a symphony is really hard. I mean there are four or five great minutes, maybe, and the rest of it for me is waffle. But, as a pianist I liked to play Chopin, because Chopin's pieces were written specially for piano and they were all beautiful melodically. I resented some of the classical music I had to play, like Bartok and stuff like that, I didn't know whether I was playing the right notes or the wrong notes. Bach I liked to play, I liked Handel very, very much. I like good musicianship, and I can appreciate someone's talent for being a good singer. For example, Johnny Mathis is an extremely good singer because of his technique, and Dionne Warwick, Sarah Vaughan and Ella Fitzgerald are wonderful singers. But you don't *have* to be a great musician to get your point across. I think Lou Reed gets his point across very well and Bob Dylan – they don't have the best voices in the world technically, but they get so much emotion. Music that is unemotional doesn't have a big effect on me. You have to have some emotion or some gift of phrasing to catch my ear.

When Rock 'n' Roll was invented, was that a major event in your life?

EJ Yeah, I remember it totally – I went to have my hair cut in the hairdressers, and I picked up a copy of *Life* magazine. There was a picture of Elvis Presley in it and, you know, I'd never seen anything like it – I remember it very vividly. That same weekend, my mum came home and said, "I've got these two fabulous records", one was *ABC Boogie* by Bill Haley and the other was *Heartbreak Hotel* by Elvis Presley. It was just weird

Elton aged

that it happened the same week, I saw him in a magazine and my mum bought the record, and that changed my life.

Did your parents ever buy you records?

EJ My dad bought me *Songs for Swinging Lovers*, by Frank Sinatra when I was about seven – I really wanted a bike so I didn't appreciate the sentiment too much. My appreciation of Sinatra grew later on. My parents divorced when I was eleven or twelve. I was very pleased when they did, because even though my father was musical, we didn't communicate that well. It was kind of strange for someone that was musical to not really want me to go ahead with the career that I actually chose. But we made up, and there are no resentments any more.

What was the first record you bought?

EJ The first 45 I ever bought, was *Reet Petite*, by Jackie Wilson, and *At the Hop*, by Danny and the Juniors. But I used to collect 78s so I think it would have been an Elvis Presley. I love the feel on some of those early records, the acoustic guitar sound was so fantastic, and they still haven't been matched today. You go into a studio and you think, let's get a sound like that one, and you never do, because they were original sounds, and it's very hard to duplicate sounds, unless you sample.

How important do you think your formal musical education was to your music writing?

EJ I thought my formal musical education was a drag at the time. I really didn't want to learn the piano properly, I was quite happy just playing in C, and G, which are the easiest keys to play as a keyboard player. But looking back on it now, it did me an awful lot of good, to learn chord structures and other keys. When I went to the Royal Academy of Music, between the ages of 11 and 15, I met a lot of people that have played on my records. Chris Thomas, who produces my records, was at the Academy with me, so our friendship goes back over thirty years. But I resented having to go to the Academy on Saturday mornings. Sometimes I used to go up to Baker Street, where the Royal Academy is, and sit on the train and go round and round the Circle line, then go home and tell my mum and dad that I'd been to the school. So, I was not the perfect student but I don't think I would have been nearly as good a musician as I am, if I hadn't had that full training.

Elton in 1965

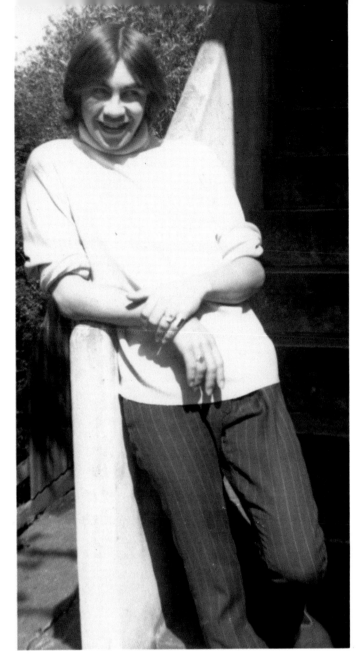

Bernie in 1968

What happened after you left school?

BT I left school when I was fifteen and worked in Lincoln in a printing press. Then I did various labouring jobs and ended up working on a chicken farm in the middle of nowhere. I was getting more and more depressed with what I was doing, to the point where I became so bored that I committed quite a lot of petty theft. So I started finding solace in my writing and of course at the same time I was obsessed with music. It was the only enjoyment that I had, aside from going out at night with my friends, getting plastered and going to work the next day. That was fun for a while but it was just getting too overbearing and I needed some other outlet. There *was* a side of me that wanted to be this rural jack-the-lad but there was also this side of me that wanted to improve my life and improve it in something that I cared about. But living where I did, there really wasn't any outlet for the local poet. The local poet where I came from was called the village idiot.

EJ The first thing I did when I left school was work in a music publishers for about a year as a tea boy – then I joined a semi-professional band called Bluesology, which later turned professional.

Do you remember meeting other up and coming musicians when you started out?

EJ Yeah, I mean we used to play at the Marquee club second on the bill to the Spencer Davis Group, Manfred Mann, the Herd, we played with Georgie Fame, Zoot Money. I remember one bill we played with Jimi Hendrix, Jimmy Jones and the Vagabonds, Jimmy Cliff and Long John Baldry, that was at the Locarno, Nottingham. I remember Fleetwood Mac playing at the Windsor Jazz festival when they were just starting out. We didn't say much to those people, because we were a very average band, we didn't really set our horizons very high, we were competent, we were able, but we weren't exactly exciting. But there are a few people that I always remember, the people that treated us nice, made an effort to say hello, they stuck in my mind. I remember Jimi Hendrix saying hello, and I thought that was really nice of him, because he didn't know me from Adam, but you know, that makes a difference for people who are up and coming. I always try and make an effort whether you like their music or whether you don't, just say hello, and try to encourage them as much as possible.

Reg Dwight had a single, why wasn't there another one?

EJ Reg Dwight had two singles with Bluesology. Reg wrote the lyrics and the music, and they were bloody awful both of them. They were first songs, you know, so they were naive but they were terribly exciting when you actually got the record in your hand, and you heard them crackling through the airwaves on Radio Luxemburg. But it was painfully obvious, that though I could write a good melody, I wasn't really a words man. I never had the confidence to write down my feelings, because my feelings have never come to the surface that much, they've always been suppressed and hidden, because I've been so shy. People think, "God, he's shy, all that extrovert business was an act?" and it kind of was, it was a way for me to say God, I can do this. But inside I was painfully shy. My feelings now are just beginning to come out, and I'm beginning to express myself a little better. But as far as writing them down as words to a song, I think that's still a long way off.

BT Elton is not a lyric writer, I don't think it's got anything to do with putting your confidence down on paper. He just doesn't do it. Some people can fix a drain, some people can't. Some people play the piano, I can't. I don't think Elton has that much desire to do it either. If you saw some of his early attempts you'd probably understand. I remember one in particular, one of the first songs that he wrote was called *The Witches' House* and it was "*I go to the witches' house, I go there whenever I can. Me and Molly Dickinson in my delivery van*". And there you have it.

Come Back Baby

Come back baby
Come back to me, yeah
And you will see, yeah
How I've changed.

'Cos you're the only love that I ever had.
You're the only love that I ever had.
Come back to me.

Come back baby
I did you wrong, yeah
And now this song I sing, I hope
Will bring you back to me.

'Cos you're the only love that I ever knew.
You're the only love that I ever knew.
Come back, come back.

Come back baby
Come back and treat me right
Come back baby
Come back I'll hold you tight.

Come back baby
Ev'ry thing is gonna be fine right now
It's gonna be fine right now
It's gonna be fine right now
'Cos you're the only love that I ever had
And you're comin' back and I am so glad
Come back to me
Come back to me

COME BACK BABY

Words and Music by REG DWIGHT

Recorded by **BLUESOLOGY** on Fontana TF 594

2/6

MILLS MUSIC LTD · MILLS HOUSE · DENMARK STREET WC 2

JUDITH DURHAM

GETTING TOGETHER

What made you want to strike out on your own away from Bluesology?

EJ I was so bored with playing cabaret. I've always said that I will not play to people who are eating fish and chips, it's a dead end for musicians. You have to earn a living, and it was a living for me, but I was just exasperated and fed up with it in the end. I really didn't know what to do, but I knew I didn't want to do that.

When and why did you move to London?

BT I moved to London when I was sixteen. I had been there before because my uncle lived in Putney and that's where I eventually stayed when I first moved there. But for the reason I went to London, I should go back to the point when I happened to be thumbing through the latest copy of *New Musical Express* and I saw this ad for a company called Liberty Records which was breaking free of EMI. They were looking for A&R guys and musicians and everything to start a new record label. And in my frustration, I thought of replying, not thinking for a minute that you could make any money at something that was so enjoyable. It was the early summer of '67 so the entire world was changing, we were all changing. Music was incredibly vital, breaking beyond the boundaries of anything that had come before, it was the time of Procul Harum, The Stones were doing *Satanic Majesty's Request*, The Beatles were doing *Sergeant Pepper*. And as a very impressionistic sixteen year old, I was writing a lot of poetry that mirrored this and I thought, well why not? Send it off and see what happens. So I sent it to Liberty Records, never dreaming that I'd ever get a reply. And here cometh the favourite

1972

story that has changed over the last two decades, about my mother mailing the letter! I don't know what my mother told you, but I don't think either of us remember the true story any more. I remember writing the letter and putting the poems in the envelope and putting it on the shelf, because somebody mailed the letters every day at the house. For some reason it got shuffled behind the clock or something; it stayed there for a couple of weeks and I think my mum saw it and said, "Oh, you forgot to post it", and she mailed it. So I can assure you that it wasn't dragged out of the wastebasket as has been suggested in various publications. Anyway the letter eventually got mailed and a reply came from Ray Williams. The thing that I liked most about the reply was that he wrote, "When you happen to be in Mayfair next, pop in and see me". Coming from the wilds of Lincolnshire, the fact that I'd be popping in to his offices on Albemarle Street in Mayfair was quite amusing. That was the thing that knocked me out most of all.

When did you first think you might be a song-writer?

BT I never thought of myself as a songwriter until the last desperate moment. I loved to write poetry, but I certainly never thought about writing songs until I saw the famous ad in *New Musical Express*.

How did you and Bernie get together?

EJ Bernie and I got together through an advert in the *New Musical Express*. Liberty Records, at that time, were being distributed by EMI Records, and they were going independent. They were looking for new talent, and I answered that advertisement. I met a guy called Ray Williams, who said, we all want to hear you sing. The only things I knew how to sing were things I used to sing in a pub, which were Jim Reeves' songs; they weren't really

looking for Jim Reeves at that time, so they weren't jumping up and down with glee at this overweight bespectacled thing looking like a lump of porridge singing a Jim Reeves song. Ray said, well, I've got all these lyrics on my desk from this guy in Lincolnshire, so I took them, and started writing music to them, without ever having met Bernie. They were very naive lyrics and they were very naive melodies, but there was a chemistry there and I enjoyed doing it. When I say lyrics, they weren't verse chorus verse chorus, they were just a page full of lyrics, which I still prefer actually. As we became more sophisticated and more knowledgeable in our songwriting, that kind of went out the window, but the early lyrics that Bernie wrote, had no iambic pentameter, they were free form, bits of verse. And I find it very easy, if there's a very long line I can make it sound short, if there's a short line I can make it sound like a long line. I just found my niche, I was very good at putting music around written words. If somebody gave me a set of lyrics I could do it no matter what, it didn't have to be Bernie, but luckily enough it was Bernie, and it was the start of an amazing relationship. Over twenty years we've never collaborated in the sense of being in the same room, and that's extraordinary for song-writers. I've never questioned it or tried to change it, because it works, I'm happy doing it, he's happy doing it.

When did you first meet Elton?

BT I met Elton, in late July of '67. I answered the ad in June of that year, and it was probably a couple of months following that when I met with Ray Williams in London. He'd had this idea (thank you Ray), this very, very good idea, of putting me together with Elton, because Elton had apparently done an audition for Liberty, which he'd failed

1972

miserably. But Ray saw some potential in him, and Elton had expressed some desire to write songs. At the same time, he admitted that on the lyrical side he wasn't too hot. Ray, remembered my lyrics and thought, OK, I'll try and put these guys together, see if something can be sparked here. He arranged for us to meet and we got together at Dick James' studio, where he was working on a session. I'd been up in London for a few weeks, a typical country boy coming to the big city, doing my perfect Dick Whittington, I had a very tatty little old suitcase, which I'm sure Elton will tell you all about, because he keeps mentioning it, and has done for the last 25 years.

EJ I remember the suitcase, it was cardboard, the original cardboard suitcase. It doesn't even constitute hand luggage these days.

BT Anyway, we met and we went round the corner to the Lancaster Grill and had a couple of cups of coffee. I passed him over the state secrets, and that, as they say, is history. I do remember one thing that proves how naive I was at the time. I was sitting in the studio waiting for him, there were several other people in there, very 'swinging London', which I was not, believe me. And there was one guy in there who was supremely cool. I was wearing a pair of sunglasses, and the guy turned to me and said, "Great shades, man, can I try them on?" And I had no idea what he was talking about. Shades? What are shades? I was totally embarrassed.

EJ I remember, he looked quite angelic and he was very young. We got on very well, he was shy, which made two of us. I really adored him from the word go, he was like the brother I never had, and it was wonderful being part of a relationship.

It was not sexual, it was not physical, but it was emotional and very loving. He was the first real friend I ever had. Over the years, we've remained best friends. I don't have to talk to him for a few months for him to still be in my life, and vice versa; he's in my heart and always will be. Since then, we've grown apart in a lot of ways, but that's necessary for friendships to last, to be different. We lived enough off each other's backs, and we've gone through that, and we've gone through living apart and being married and being crazy, and being drunk, and being miserable, and being happy. We've gone through all those, and we're still together. And I love him more than I've ever done.

BT Elton and I got on immediately. Not with the intensity that it became later on, but we did find a natural affinity, partly because we were both loners. I was a loner because I was a country boy in the big city, so I was a little out of my depth, and although Elton had been around the block, he'd toured and he'd clubbed with major American artists, and seen a lot of things, I still think he was fairly naive, and certainly a loner. He didn't have a vast circle of friends. So, that drew us together but we also saw in each other differences which complemented each other. We learned a lot from each other immediately, I taught him about a social order that he wasn't aware of, and vice versa. He drew me into things that I was not aware of on a musical level. The radical differences have always been the thing that drew us together in the end.

How did you come to live with Elton and his mother?

BT When I first went down to London I was living with my aunt in Putney, who took great care of me, looked after me, fed me, but that could only

"I'd just been appointed as head of Artists and Repertoire for Liberty Records. My job was to find talent – recording artists. So I put an ad in *New Musical Express*. I had hundreds and hundreds of letters responding. One of them was from Elton and I called him up and asked him to come and see me in my swish office. And there was this charming shy overweight little fella, called Reg. I recall him saying that he was singing with Long John Baldry and Bluesology. He was upset that Long John wouldn't allow him to sing very much other than backing vocals. I felt quite sorry for this chap, so we carried on talking. I asked him a bit more about his abilities, and he said: "Well, I'm really a singer and a keyboard player, but I don't write lyrics". We went over to the piano, and he started to play a few things. I decided to go and make some demos with him. The first tape was a Jim Reeves song, I can't remember the other things but I always hung on to the demo tape.

Also in this sack of letters was one from a chap called Bernie Taupin. He said he was, basically, a poet, but felt that his poems, could be set to music, could I help him? I remembered this chap called Reg, and I thought well maybe I'll pass the poems on. So I sent Elton some lyrics, and they began exchanging these by post, and that's how they started writing.

I thought of putting those two together, out of all the hundreds, because I actually had some feeling for them. I felt they had an ability, I mean Bernie would probably look at those lyrics now and laugh but there was

something. And with Elton, I loved his voice, he had a super voice, there was no question about it. It didn't matter what he looked like at that time. It was just a gut reaction – let's put them together.

The first time Elton and Bernie met we went for a drink. That was a very grown up thing to do in those days, and they hit it off straight away. They were like an old couple. It was obvious that they got on very well together, they didn't get in each other's way. I think that was the secret, Bernie didn't want to be a singer or play the piano, and Elton really couldn't write the lyrics, so it just fitted; they respected each other's position."

Ray Williams

1972

really last for a bit because I had to be closer to Elton. It was really important for our writing, for us to be in the same place. Eventually, Elton took up with this girl, and the three of us all moved into an apartment in Islington, which everybody told us was to become the new Chelsea. It never did, and I don't think it ever has. But we believed them, and we moved in. We started to work but eventually it sort of crash-landed, and we ended up moving lock, stock and barrel back to Elton's mother's house. That's where we started doing the best of our earliest work. I would spend day after day writing; that's when we really started to enjoy writing.

> "Bernie was a very deep thinking, very quiet person. He used to love to sit up in the trees outside the flat, and write lyrics up there."
>
> *Elton's Mum*

EJ We both lived in the same room in bunk beds at my mother's flat, in Northwood Hills. We had all our records in there, all our clothes. God knows how we did it, but it was great fun, I mean those years were tremendous, I look back on them and I get very nostalgic about how much fun we did have. There were very fierce arguments too, probably because I'd never had that close a relationship with anybody before, so I was very possessive and I used to get jealous when he had to go back to Lincolnshire. You'd think, oh Christ, you must have got on each other's nerves, but we really didn't. We were very young, we went through tremendous enjoyment and tremendous hope. That tremendous hope when someone's going to do your song, and you count on it, and then the despair if they say, no, they're not going

to do it. We went through incredible depressions and frustrations. My mother and stepfather, to their credit, were always very supportive, and they said, "Well if you don't like it, you can always go and get a job up the greengrocers", and our frustration soon dissipated because we still loved what we were doing.

Elton and Bernie at Frome Court with Elton's mum, his auntie Win and two neighbours

Do you think you were the brother that he never had?

BT Yeah, I think so, and vice versa, because I never really associated with my elder brother. My younger brother came much later on; he was only seven when I went to London. I had friends that I regarded as my brothers, and I was very close to them, but Elton was a whole different kettle of fish. I admired the fact that he'd worked the clubs, he'd been around, he'd worked with all these major American artists, people like Billy Stewart, Major Lance and Patti LaBelle, and all these great people that I'd listened to. I was impressed by that, and also the fact that he was a musician and the possibility of him being able to work with something that I'd written, that was exciting. So all of those things together kept us pretty tight.

Did you share similar music influences, did you like the same music when you met?

EJ I don't think we did like the same music, I mean we had a basic appreciation of Rock 'n' Roll, but he turned me on to Dylan, and I turned him on to some other things. There were so many great albums to buy, in the late sixties and early seventies, that we used to spend a lot on imports. In those days, you could buy maybe seven or eight albums a week that were really tremendous albums, now you're lucky to find seven or eight singles in a year. But in those days it was different, music was exciting and much more fun.

You're both very avid record collectors?

BT Saying that Elton and I are avid record collectors is an understatement. That's the fuel for everything we've ever done and we're still the fans we always were. When somebody at a record company or an artist says I'll get you a copy of a new album, we say – no way. We'll buy it, because that's what it's all about. There's an artist out there trying to make a living and usually it's a new artist. I want to go out and buy his record. I want him to make his five cents, I want him to be able to make more records if I like it. There was one point where we would buy everything that came out. I remember

1972

one time when Elton and I went on tour for three months. I left word with the record store to keep a copy of every album that comes in, because I wanted it for my record collection and I didn't want to miss out on anything. Big mistake. I came back and there were cases and cases of records. I had Vince Hill records, I had Matt Monroe records. I had everything, it was unbelievable.

One of the most enjoyable times for Elton and me in those idyllic summer days in the late sixties was hanging out at Music Land. The guys that ran Music Land became very good friends of ours and Elton worked there in his spare time occasionally. We used to go and spend the day there. That was our drug, a healthy one, I might add. The most exciting thing was waiting for the imports to come in. We were obsessed by American records, not just because of what was inside them but we loved the covers, we loved the card on American records because it was harder, they didn't have that glossy sheen that English records had. It's funny how later we met American artists who used to hang out and wait for English imports because they liked the glossy sheen and the thin card. I remember Elton and I waiting for *Electric Ladyland* to arrive for hours and hours late into the night. We didn't have that much money either; Elton was making slightly more than I was. He used to say "We don't need to buy a copy each, I'll buy a copy and you can play mine". And I'd say "Elton, I don't intend living with you forever. Nice thought, but I think we're going to want to have our own places at some point!" I've still got records that have my initials written in the top right hand corner in biro – "B.T.", we used to mark them. We used to keep them on each side of the room, he had his side of the room and I had my side of the room. Elton used to collect all those weekly magazines like *The History of the First World War* and *Plant Life for Our Times* and *The*

History of the British Locomotive. He had them all bound so his side of the room was a little more filled up than mine.

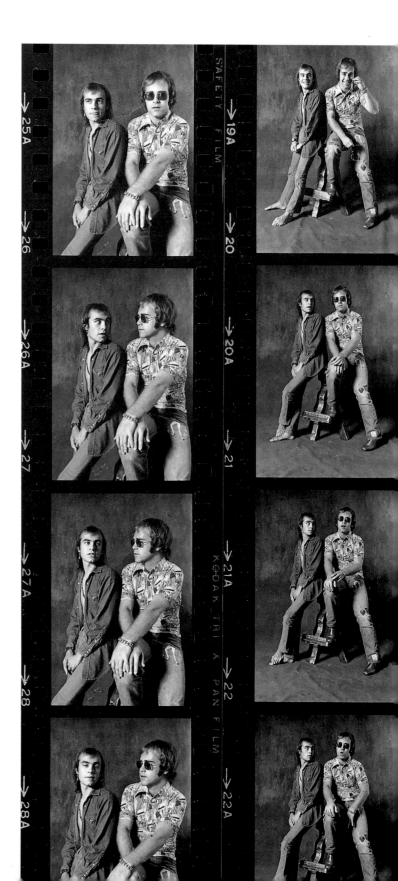

Can you describe what it was like living and working together?

BT It was a bit like a student dormitory. Elton and I

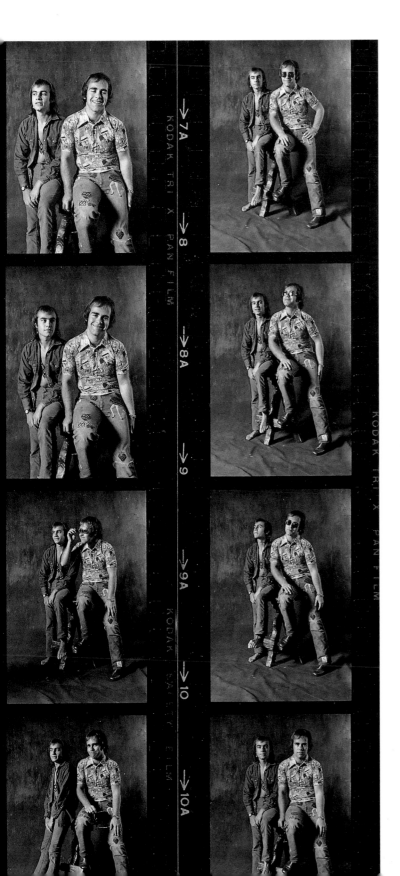

shared a bedroom. We had bunk beds and it was crammed with every possible piece of our paraphernalia. Elton had one side of the room and I had the other. During the day I'd write in there. The living room was at the end of the hallway, with the piano in it, so I would walk down and put something on the piano for Elton, then I'd go back and write some more and he would work on it and then I'd hear the shout – "Come and take a listen". What made it so great was that there was so much spirit and so much love for what we were doing and so much excitement. The music of the time also inspired us because when we met and started sharing an apartment together we listened to everything. We turned each other on to music. Elton turned me on to a lot of R & B and Motown stuff while I was turning him on to more folk-orientated stuff like Tim Hardin, Bob Dylan and Leonard Cohen. A lot of those early lyrics that we wrote on the *Elton John* album like *Sixty Years On* and *The King Must Die* were inspired not only by music but also by what I was reading at the time; Mary Renault inspired *The King Must Die*. The music, the poetry, whether it was Tolkien, whether it was C. S. Lewis, they were all thrown into the pot.

> "They used to wait for me at the window and as soon as I got in it was "Come and listen to this, come and listen to this". If it was one I cried at, they'd say well that's a winner, we'll have that one."
>
> *Elton's Mum*

Swan Queen of the Laughing Lake

are falling faster from the mirror of my mind,
concieve the troubles of the truths I leave behind.
false beliefs upon the people there who stood,
a fountain in the burning cedar wood.
ting faulty visions in the mirarge of your soul,
belief along the crooked rabbit holes.

f simple Simons church will ring out on the hill,
ds will laugh along with the golden daffodils.
s and the clowns will light the bright beacons that burn
wan queen of the laughing lake returns,
wan queen of the laughing lake returns.

ve and negative have never really shown,
ings from heaven or o   known.
n us simple thoughts.
mortal people canno
l stand along the ri
ase you may hounour u

ple Simons ch
ugh alon
w

TARTAN-COLOURED

grass in Ashfield Park is dy
everybody dreams of deeds
tartan-coloured lady walk
tartan-coloured lady she is

k of willow trees

(F)

The Year of the Teddy Bear.

F   Dm   Db Ab   Bb.
We have raised all our glasses to great men who've gone,
but the greatest of all is the unmentioned one.   Ditto
He's the king of the cupboard the ruler of toy's   Gm - Bb
now he will celebrate with all girls and boys.
                                                    F - Dm - D

of the Teddy Bears come,
ked under the sun.

time and between,
gone into a dream.
in June,
in balloons,
in the sky

stic flowers
for hours and hours and hou

he Teddy Bears come,
walked under the sun.

to four thousand,
ion now.
front of the fishmongers ware
disspose of this troublesome be
nd its now

of the Teddy Bears come,
ver walked under the sun.

A Dandelion Dies in the Wind.

I   See my eyes and see my arms
    the seagulls say you've gone,
    it was just a game of lets pretend
    and Ill whistle to the waves that lend me tears.

Purple clouds,
golden rain
yesterday has gone,
and a dandelion dies in the wind.

If your quick enough to rise
with the sleep still in your eyes
you'll see the shadow of the sun above my mind.
For the sea of tears is drowning me
I cannot feel, I cannot see
I Know that only you can help me now.

Purple clouds,
olden rain
sterday has gone,
d a dandelion dies in the wind.

a dandelion sighs and he trys to tell the wind
cryings not a bad thing
worrying is a sin.
ey sent a cloud from heaven
d ride into the skies
ape all of my troubles
cast away your lies.
rains have turned to gold
ds of yesterday
delion dies in

Am
D Em
F - C   b
Bb E F

GMBb C
Am G
D Am F - C
Am G C G
Dm Am F C
Bb G
Dm Bb
Cf G

F C
D G

A Bb
Dm Bb

I GUESS I'LL READ THE
AND PLAY MARBLES
AND

Can you remember any of your very early lyrics?

BT I don't know if I remember any of the actual lyrics. But I know they were very derivative. If The Beatles wrote "Being for the Benefit of Mr. Kite", then I'd write something that had the same connotations. I remember we wrote things like *The Year of the Teddy Bear*, *A Dandelion Dies in the Wind*. There were some really esoteric ones: *Swan Queen of the Laughing Lake*, I remember that one – that was a great one. *Tartan Coloured Lady*, *Colour Slide City*, I mean they were all terrible rip-offs of everything.

1973

Elton, Nigel Olsson and Dee Murray 1970

EARLY CAREER

Elton and Bernie with Dick James and his son Stephen 1972

What was the first job you got together?

EJ We were signed originally to the Hollies' music company, which was Gralto. That didn't work out, I don't think they even realised we were signed to them! And then we signed to Dick James Music. Dick was kind of like a grandfather or a father to us in a way, he did a lot for us. Our relationship ended up in court, which I always regret, but I have to state here and now, if it hadn't been for Dick, we wouldn't have ever got where we are. I don't think he understood our music that much, but it didn't matter, whenever we were in trouble financially, or when we needed something, he was always there. A big big part of being signed to Dick was the prestige. At that time he had the Beatles, the Mamas and the Papas, Roger Cook and Roger Greenaway, and a lot of really big writers in this country as well.

How did you come to be involved with Dick James?

BT When I met Elton up at the Dick James studio, we were not involved with Dick James. We were initially signed to a company that Ray Williams had, called Gralto. But Dick found out we were moonlighting demos in his studio. One day there was a purge in the office and the office manager busted us for it, and we were hauled up before the headmaster! Dick offered us a songwriting contract, and being the naive youths that we were, we fell upon it like thieves. So we were put on a retainer and we started churning out songs. It got a little demoralising after a while because Dick, bless his heart, kept saying these songs are a little esoteric. So we were pushed into writing commercial material for other people. They were trying to get us to write songs for the stock top 40 people who at that time were very dependent on songwriters. People like Tom Jones, Englebert Humperdink, Cilla Black and Lulu were very dominant in the charts back then. We had no qualms at first because we were getting paid, and getting paid to write songs wasn't too bad because I could be driving a tractor or shovelling dead chickens into an incinerator. So it was okay up to a point but we weren't having much success at it. We weren't getting covers by the score, in fact I don't know if we got any. Then this guy called Steve Brown turned up at the office and stumbled upon us which was pretty easy to do because we were always there. Steve started listening to some of our stuff and came up with this great notion, why don't you forget what Dick's saying, don't

take any notice of anybody else, just do what you want to do. I'll take care of Dick, just write the songs that you want to write. And we did. The first thing we wrote was *Skyline Pigeon* which turned out to be the most successful thing we'd done up to that point. It was covered by two people and got a lot of airplay. It wasn't a hit but looking back on it it's still a pretty good song. It has a lot of pretention to it but hell, you are pretentious when you're sixteen or seventeen years old and in 1967, everyone was pretentious. From that song, songwriting became our bread and butter and then Reg became Elton and we started making our own records.

It was around this time that you became Elton John. Why did you do that?

EJ Elton John was the person that Reg Dwight always wanted to be. I was always uncomfortable with my name as a kid, Reg, Reginald, you know, it's a very middle class name in England, I mean how can you call a baby in your arms "My little Reg here"? I mean it's just not a young person's name. I couldn't wait to change it.

"Elton's first official gig as Elton John was at The Speakeasy Club, with Nigel Olsson and Dee Murray. I was a bit sceptical about it happening with just that line-up, but it really did, it cooked, it was marvellous. We invited everybody along. I consider that one of the first important venues, and we got a lot of publicity."

Ray Williams

How did it feel the first time you saw one of your songs on vinyl?

BT One of my earliest recollections of working with Elton was the first song we ever wrote together called *Scarecrow*. It was literally the first marriage of my lyric to Elton's melody, and in those days everything went from tape to acetate which was a very archaic way of making demo records. They took these acrylics and carved the music into the disc. It was great to watch them being made because you saw your music going from the needle into the groove, being carved in there. I was living with my aunt in Putney and I remember going home with this acetate of *Scarecrow*. I just played it over and over again thinking wow, this is living man, this is really what it's all about. So you can imagine how I felt when I got our first 45. Interestingly enough, the first Elton single ever released, I didn't write although I was credited as writer on it. It was called *I've Been Loving You* and was pressured by Dick. I remember being at Ray Williams' house when it came out. It was going to be played on Radio 1, and we sat around a table, around this little transistor radio, waiting for it to come on. It wasn't particularly wonderful but it was a step in the right direction. I suppose the first hit record that really represented us was *Lady Samantha*. That was exciting, it was a good record and got a lot of air play and again, running home with that was exciting. But I still get excited when I get a pressing of something we do now.

Were you disappointed when I Can't Go On Living Without You *failed to become the British entry for the 1969 Eurovision Song Contest?*

EJ Not really, I mean, *I Can't Go On Living Without You* was a song that was written really by me, I wrote the lyrics as well. It was down as John and Taupin, because *I've Been Loving You* was exactly

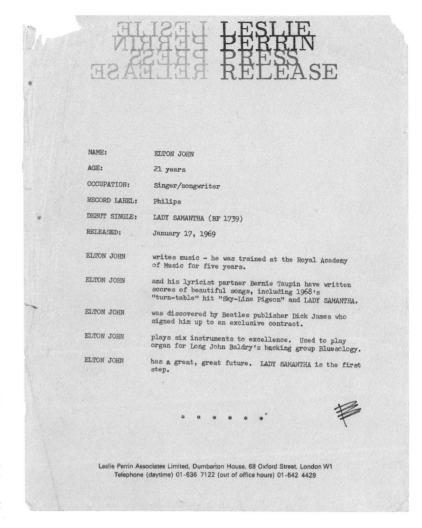

the same song. You can tell those two songs apart because the lyrics to *I Can't Go On Living Without You* are just so awful. It was exciting to have a song in the last six of the Eurovision Song Contest, as far as the British entry was concerned. And to say that we weren't excited would be a downright lie, of course we were excited. It came last, and it got its just desserts. But anything at that point, when you haven't made it, – any bit of publicity, or anyone thinking of covering your song, it was what you lived for, it's what kept you going; the hope that one day someone would have a hit with one of your songs.

What was your first successful record?

EJ *Lady Samantha* which was produced by Steve Brown. I always remember because it was in B

Elton with his mother and stepfather

38

Flat and the B Flat of the electric piano that we hired was out of tune, so I had to play a song in B Flat without playing the B Flats, which is rather difficult. It got us a lot of radio play, and it was the first record where people started to hear my name.

What were your feelings when your first album came out?

EJ *Empty Sky*. I just couldn't believe it when *Empty Sky* came out. There was an advert for it in the *International Times*, which was a magazine of that time. It was *very* exciting to have an album out. *Empty Sky* is still one of my favourite albums and it had one great song on it, which was *Skyline Pigeon*.

Who were the sort of people who were buying your early albums?

EJ Well, *Elton John* was the album that really launched me. At that time the recording industry was going through so many changes and we used to buy records to listen to the sound of how the drums were recorded, the piano was recorded, and the bass. It's not easy to get a good sound on the road, or it never used to be, and people like Leon Russell helped change that, and I helped change that by using different pick ups. I think the people that bought our records were totally into sounds. *Elton John* was very much a mixture of wonderful rhythm tracks, I mean without the Buckmaster arrangements, that album would have been nowhere near as good as it was. Those arrangements were so unique; not just boring string arrangements, but orchestral arrangements, with funky type songs.

When did you get the first inkling that you were both onto something?

EJ I think when we were making the *Elton John* album, and *Border Song* came out as a single, and got enormous play on the radio.

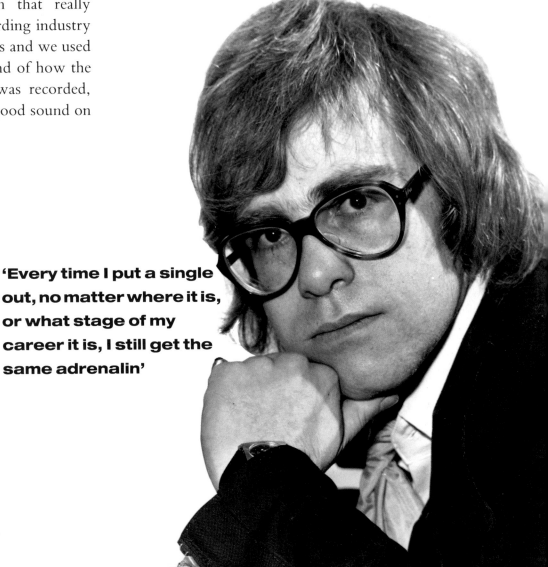

'Every time I put a single out, no matter where it is, or what stage of my career it is, I still get the same adrenalin'

Did you and Bernie ever bet about making it before you did?

EJ No, we were very naive and we were still in awe. I remember Three Dog Night recorded *Lady Samantha* and *Your Song*, and they had two big hit albums in America. They came to Britain and played the Marquee club, and I remember picking up Danny Hutton who was one of the singers and taking him round. We couldn't believe that he phoned us up from America to say hi. That was quite extraordinary to have a song on a hit album in America. I mean I used to buy the Billboard chart and underline it. The things that were happening were really beyond our dreams but luckily we didn't get big-headed about it, because we were playing with too many good musicians on stage. I remember playing with Derek and the Dominos, on their first American tour when

> *"*I was going to New York to tour, as Derek of Derek and the Dominos and everyone was going crazy about this kid called Elton John. I was slightly threatened by all this, when I heard that this guy had a hit album and everyone loved it. Anyway, somehow or other we got hooked up and we played this tour of America together, and gradually, I got to know him, and I realised that he was a really nice man, and very humble. I had this thing where I wanted to be anonymous, but at the same time I did want to blow people off the stage so I was working double hard and to go on after Elton – I mean I wouldn't do it now, not many people would, but even then it was a big challenge.*"*
>
> *Eric Clapton*

Layla and the album *Derek and the Dominos* had come out, and we were second on the bill. Eric Clapton at that point didn't want any publicity about being in the band. I think the album *Derek* wasn't a big hit until two or three years after it came out. People didn't know who Derek and the Dominos were because of Eric's reticence about being the star name in a band. We had some wonderful shows with Eric.

Your first chart success was Your Song. *Did you know it was a hit when you recorded it?*

EJ No. I never know what's gonna be a hit. I haven't got that ability to pick out a hit song. Some things jump out at you straight away, *Don't Go Breaking My Heart*, was one of them. But I mean things like *Your Song* I didn't think could be a hit, or *Bennie & The Jets*. There was a point in my career where I could have released anything and it would have been a hit. . . But some songs that we've written that I thought would be hits weren't. *Cry to Heaven* for example, on the *Ice on Fire* album. And some of the songs that I didn't think would be hits have been hits. And that's been good for me in a way, because nothing's worse than someone who's cocksure. Every time I put a single out, no matter where it is, or what stage of my career it is, I still get the same adrenalin, and I'm still ringing up to see what the sales figures are. When it does do something – I mean for example when *Sacrifice* was a big hit last year, and went to my first solo number one in England, I was extremely excited. I didn't see that as being a hit single either. When I wrote that song in Denmark I remember people in the studio saying oh that's a hit, and I thought, I don't know about that, but it's a nice song. But that's a quality I've managed to retain. No matter how blasé one has become or unhappy one's been, when you've got a record out there, it's exciting.

WRITING AND COMPOSITION

Can you tell me how you write your songs?

BT That's a very hard question to answer. I know so many people that do it so many different ways, and the way that Elton and I do it is so different from the way anybody else does it. Simply, I write the lyrics, I present them to him, he writes the melody, we get together and listen, we go into the studio and we cut the record, that's the simple version. How I come up with the ideas, that's something else. I'm inspired by titles, and if I write anything down beforehand, it's usually titles or first lines. I always find titles very interesting – they're invigorating, you can bounce off titles. When I was younger and I went into a record store, if the song titles were interesting, if they stretched themselves beyond *My Heart Got Broken*, or *I Love You*, or *She Broke My Heart*, then I'd tend to be more interested in the record. But I always strive to find something interesting to write about.

> "I think it's horses for courses. If Elton feels that he doesn't write as good a lyric as Bernie or Bernie doesn't write music, then I think it's a perfect combination. If you know your weakness and you can find someone else that has that strength that's the way to do it."
>
> *Phil Collins*

> "It really doesn't involve them spending any time together because as long as the lyrics are there, Elton can just take the lyrics. Because it's two instead of one, it's twice as strong."
>
> *Neil Young*

1970

45

1973

Your Song

It's a little bit funny, this feeling inside
I'm not one of those, who can easily hide,
I don't have much money, but boy if I did
I'd buy a big house where we both could live.

If I was a sculptor, but then again no,
Or a man who makes potions in a travelling show
I know it's not much, but it's the best I can do
My gift is my song and this one's for you.

And you can tell everybody, this is your song
It may be quite simple but now that it's done,
I hope you don't mind, I hope you don't mind
That I put down in words
How wonderful life is while you're in the world

I sat on the roof and kicked off the moss
Well a few of the verses, well they've got me quite cross
But the sun's been quite kind while I wrote this song,
It's for people like you, that keep it turned on.

So excuse me forgetting, but these things I do
You see I've forgotten, if they're green or they're blue
Anyway the thing is, what I really mean
Yours are the sweetest eyes I've ever seen.

You don't really tend to write conventional love songs . . .

BT No, I certainly never try to write a conventional love song. The essence of boredom is the conventional love song, the standard top 40 MOR. Who wants to hear a happy love song? That's so boring. Love songs should be all about broken hearts and darkness and sadness. Songs are about people listening to them and relating to them. When I was a teenager, I used to listen to Gene Pitney and Del Shannon and say this is my song of the week as my heart was broken yet again at school. I've always been attracted to the dark side. I mean I love darkness, I love sex. People point out that a lot of our songs have been written about hookers and strippers, what can I tell you, I'm

46

'I'm inspired by titles, and if I write anything down beforehand, it's usually titles or first lines'

fascinated. I've always been drawn to that side of life. There's far more fascination for me in the underbelly of society rather than the green grass and white picket fence. Do you remember the scene at the beginning of *Blue Velvet* when you see the worms underneath the earth and then they come up and show the garden and the guy mowing the lawn. Well I'm under the ground. That's where I find my ideas, from the dark side. The dark side's more interesting.

What would you say typifies a Bernie Taupin song?

BT One of the nicest compliments I'm often paid is that the content of our songs is very cinematic. There are a lot of subjects that seem to crop up in the lyrics, and I think one of the things that people have possibly not given us credit for is that we touched on subjects that were thought of as being a little risqué long before other people did. Whether they were about hookers or drugs, I think we conjured up some interesting characters in our songs, you know, there are some that are almost like little, mini novels.

But I don't think there's anybody who's been more diverse than us, I mean, we've done everything, we've done country, we've done blues songs, we've done pure pop, we've done reggae, I mean we've tried everything, you know, we've not always done it well – for the most part at least it's been interesting.

"Bernie's lucky that he's got an outlet for his talent, he's lucky that he doesn't have to rely on a book publisher. I mean it's a wonderful thing to have Elton as your voice."

Eric Clapton

"I've sung *Come Down In Time* since *Tumbleweed Connection* came out. I learnt to play it on the guitar and I used to perform it in the clubs, so I know it. Its a beautiful song. I love Bernie's lyrics, its one of those songs you wished you'd written. I love the line: *. . . a cluster of nightjars sang some songs out of tune.* It creates some very evocative images. It's a strange story. I think everyone has their own version of what it could be about. When I came to record it for the tribute album I just had Elton play piano and I played double bass. You can see the skeleton of the song better if you put less into it. And that shows the strength of a song if you can sing it with one instrument."

Sting

Elton and Sting

Sting said he wished he'd written Come Down in Time, *do you ever feel that about songs?*

BT I hear songs all the time that I wish I'd written. I'm sure Sting's written a few of them too. I see performers that not only do I wish I'd written their songs, I wish I was them, I want to be there now, I want to have that intensity, I want to be that person. But more often than not it's actually lines in songs. Don Henley writes great lines. Sting writes great lines, there's a lot of great songwriters out right now.

Come Down In Time
In the quiet silent seconds I turned off the light switch
And I came down to meet you in the half light the moon left
While a cluster of night jars sang some songs out of tune
A mantle of bright light shone from a room

Come down in time I still hear her say
So clear in my ear like it was today
Come down in time was the message she gave
Come down in time and I'll meet you half way

Well I don't know if I should have heard her as yet
But a true love like hers is a hard love to get
And I've walked most all the way and I ain't heard her call
And I'm getting to thinking if she's coming at all

Come down in time I still hear her say
So clear in my ear like it was today
Come down in time was the message she gave
Come down in time and I'll meet you half way

There are women and women, and some hold you tight
While some leave you counting the stars in the night

What sort of state were Bernie's lyrics in when you eventually got them?

EJ They were hand-written lyrics and they weren't in any real shape or form, which I still prefer. He would give them to me at Frome Court or I would get them through the post from Lincolnshire, and I would go into the living room, 'write' them on the upright piano and then come back and play them to him. That's where we wrote *Your Song*, that's where we wrote the whole *Elton John* album basically, and we write really

quickly. We don't write all year long, we write when we want to do a record. And that's always been the case, except occasionally when we've done one-off singles. I go in there with a batch of lyrics, and whatever lyric catches my eye, I start on that one and then off I go. Usually the song is

finished in less than an hour from my point of view. A lot of the albums like *Yellow Brick Road* for example, were written in a couple of days. I write very, very quickly. There can be quite a challenge in going to the studio with nothing written. With the *Sleeping With The Past* album. I went to Denmark with the lyrics, went into the studio, and we had the backing track down within a couple of hours.

"It's such a weird relationship, Bernie writes the lyrics and sends them off and gets a song back. That is extraordinary to me."

Roger Daltry

"Elton's music always seemed to come from that R&B root. His left hand would set up the groove, and Bernie's lyrics would give him the emotional angle that made the rest of the music grow."

Eric Clapton

Are you a disciplined writer?

BT I'm very lazy as a writer. When Elton and I first started working together, that's all we did – write songs. We were in each other's company continually and we forged our craft. But as we grew older and lived further apart, we both became proficient in other things. I haven't written a song in a year. I'm about to start writing some stuff with Elton, but we needed a little time off. People would like to think that I'm continually buried in some quiet corner, writing songs, but we don't do it like that. People sometimes hold it against us that we're very instant in the way that we write, it comes to both of us very quickly. If it doesn't, then it's not working, it's not flowing. When Elton sits down

with something I've given him, if nothing comes to him, then he'll go on to something else. He doesn't take my lyrics, read them, and thoroughly analyse them and say, I see this in here, and I see that in there. Maybe there are times that I've thought he should read through my stuff before he starts work, but he doesn't do that, he puts them down and it's very instant for him. But the songs have stood the test of time, they've proved their immortality. I know people, and I respect them, who spend months working on one song, they'll come back to it, rewrite it, and come up with a great song. We can write a song within the space of an hour, and I think it's equally as good, it will stand the test of time, just as much as a song that took two months to create.

Do you always understand his lyrics?

EJ No. I don't understand some of the lyrics, especially the early ones; *Take Me to the Pilot*, I've no idea what that's about, nor does he. Some of the early ones were written when, you know, we had 'newspaper taxis' and things like that. We were tradesmen learning our craft and we were influenced by what other people were writing. There were some really great song writers around, like Jagger and Richards, Lennon and McCartney, Leon Russell, Paul Simon, Joni Mitchell. Plus the classic songwriters – Goffin and King and Lieber and Stoller and people like that. So we were influenced by what we heard from other people, and we copied, until we found a style of our own.

BT We all write things but don't know what they mean, we pretend that we do, but again, that's great fun. I would say of at least fifty to sixty percent of the early stuff that Elton and I did, lyrically I'd no idea what I was writing, and I'm sure Dylan did the same thing. Not that I'm putting myself in the same bracket, but Dylan had fun with words, and that's what it's all about, stringing words together. I used to hear a story about David Bowie throwing words into a hat, picking them out and putting them together. The great revolutionary poets did that; I'm sure Baudelaire and Rimbaud were so stoned out of their minds, they just threw things together and went wow! – that sounds good. It's how they sound together, you don't have to worry whether it rhymes or whether the meter's great, it's just how it feels here and now. The perfect example of that is *Take Me to the Pilot*. If anybody can tell me what that song's about it'd be great. But hey, it worked.

1971

Take Me To The Pilot

If you feel that it's real
I'm on trial
And I'm here in your prison
Like a coin in your mint
I am dented and spent with high treason

Through a glass eye, your throne
Is the one danger zone
Take me to the Pilot for control
Take me to the Pilot of your soul
Take me to the Pilot
Lead me to his chamber
Take me to the pilot
I am but a stranger.

Na, na, na, na, etc.

Well I know he's not old and I'm told he's a virgin
For he may be she
But what I'm told is never for certain.

Through a glass eye, your throne
Is the one danger zone
Take me to the Pilot for control
Take me to the Pilot of your soul
Take me to the Pilot
Lead me to his chamber
Take me to the Pilot
I am but a stranger.

Na, na, na, na, etc.

Do you get irritated by people's interpretation of your lyrics?

BT No, it's like books, it's like movies, they should be open to interpretation. My favourite one is *Madman Across The Water*; it was the time of Watergate and everybody thought that the *Madman Across The Water* was Nixon in the White House. It's the same with songs. In the early days people spent a lot of time trying to interpret our songs, and sometimes not positively. People seem to find anti-Christian and anti-Semitic messages. If anything they may be a little anti-Christian, because growing up a Catholic, I've had my anger with the Church, but I always try to put positive messages in songs.

> "I covered *The Bitch Is Back* once on a rough album of mine and I opened my show with it in the 70s. The attitude of the song was right for me. It's a great entrance number. I was doing the hotel circles then and it was a little bit shocking for that crowd."
>
> *Tina Turner*

Do you enjoy hearing other people singing your songs?

BT I love it – I mean, our songs are so open to interpretations. I don't want people to take our songs and make them sound like us, I want them to take them and do what the hell they want with them. They can turn them into rap records, they can turn them into speed metal, I'd love that, it's what it's all about.

> "*Burn Down The Mission* captures what Elton was doing at the time of *Tumbleweed Connection*, which I liked a lot when I first heard it. When we came to record it for the tribute album, we sat listening to Elton's version just to pick out the bits we wanted to use and it was amazing how loose it was. It's only recently that things have become so finely tuned. It reminded us how loose those early records were – it still had a magic to it."
>
> *Phil Collins*

How do you feel when you hear Sinatra singing a song of yours, like he did at the Albert Hall?

EJ Yeah I went to see Frank Sinatra at the Albert Hall with Bernie and he sang *Sorry Seems To Be The Hardest Word*. There are certain people that have charisma, that can walk into a room and have got it more than other people. Sinatra is one of them.

Bernie and I started out writing songs for other people, but we weren't very good at it, in fact we were lousy at it. Hardly anybody recorded those songs. So we ended up writing our own things to please ourselves, and then people started to record them. But I don't care who it is I've always thought it was a big compliment when anybody recorded your song, no matter what version they

Bernie and Frank Sinatra

'Bernie and I started out writing songs for other people but we weren't very good at it, so we ended up writing our own things to please ourselves'

1973

did of it. I've always been disappointed that no one's ever had a hit with one of my songs. The nearest I've come to it was *Border Song* sung by Aretha Franklin, in America, which got into the twenties in 1970. The other one was sung by Arthur Mullard and Hilda Baker, two English comedians, who did a cover version of *Don't Go Breaking My Heart*. So I mean, the spectrum between Aretha Franklin and those two is quite amazing. Bernie's had much more success. It was necessary for him to branch out and write with other people, because I don't think that if it had just been the two of us, the relationship would have been really stretched. He's achieved far more in that field than I have, and I envy that, because it's great to have a hit song written by you and recorded by someone else.

Did he comment after he'd read some of your lyrics?

BT Elton's very reserved with his comments on my material. He tends to make critiques of them much later on. When I give him something, I don't think he even reads through it before he works on it. He puts it on the piano and he takes it from top to bottom. I can't remember a time when he called me up and said, God I love this batch of lyrics. More recently he seems to be getting into my work, he's looking back on the body of our work, and appreciating it more. There are songs that we've written together where he's finished the whole track off, recorded it, called me up and said God I didn't realise what this song's about, I really love these lyrics, but I don't take compliments very well; I get a little embarrassed by anybody that gives me any sort of pat on the back.

Have you ever been disappointed with what he's done with your lyrics?

BT No, I've been surprised at times. But when I write

something it usually says what kind of song it should be. If I write the lyric for a song like *Sacrifice*, you know that it's probably not going to be a full tilt Rock 'n' Roll song, because it doesn't express those emotions.

Sacrifice

It's a human sign
When things go wrong
When the scent of her lingers
And temptations strong.

In to the boundry
Of each married man
Sweet deceit comes callin'
And negativity lands.

Cold cold heart
Hard done by you
Some things look better baby
Just passin' through

And it's no sacrifice
Just a simple word
It's two hearts living
In two separate worlds
But it's no sacrifice
No sacrifice
It's no sacrifice at all.

Mutual misunderstanding
After the fact
Sensitivity builds a prison
In the final act.

We lose direction
No stone unturned
No tears to damn you
When jealousy burns.

Cold cold heart
Hard done by you
Somethings look better baby
Just passing through.

And it's no sacrifice
Just a simple word
It's two hearts living
In two separate worlds.
But it's no sacrifice
No sacrifice
It's no sacrifice at all.

Cold cold heart
Hard done by you
Some things look better baby
Just passing through.

If you write *Saturday Night's Alright for Fighting*, you know it's not a ballad. I've become much more controlled in my writing over the years. I don't necessarily think that's good, I'd like to go back to a more free form style, and I think Elton would like to do that too. But you can't deny the fact that as you grow older, you get more professional. I'd like to experiment with some other things, but I'm not a seventeen-year-old kid off of the farm anymore, you know, and he's not a seventeen-year-old kid from the suburbs of London. When we record again I've got a feeling that we'll probably do something incredibly esoteric. When I first started writing songs, before I met up with Elton, I had no structure in mind, I was very free form. I didn't know anything about playing music, when I was sixteen. But Elton is the most musical person I've ever met, it vibrates from him. He's one of the finest musicians in the world. He's never given the credit for it, but he is. You can't be around somebody like that for as long as I've been around him, and not have his musicality rub off. And whereas when I wrote, early on, I just wrote free form, now it's almost impossible for me to write unless I've a guitar on my lap, then I can play my chords and it gives me a structure. Elton would probably like me to throw that guitar in the fire and do something more oblique.

Do you ever alter his lyrics much?

EJ Yes. Sometimes. There are some verses that have been crossed out, like in *Daniel*, which led to people not understanding the song. The last verse explained everything, but it just made the song too long. There are lines that I cross out because they don't work, and sometimes I use the chorus as the verse and the verse as the chorus. He's always given me carte blanche to do that, he's never complained. There have been situations where he hasn't heard the song until the record's finished and that must be quite a shock. I know there are things he's written that he intended to be ballads and I've turned into other songs but he's never really complained. I would think he's happy with most of the things I've written, not all of them, that would be impossible, but I would say eighty per cent of the lyrics that he's given me, he's been pleased with the end result. I'm hazarding a guess because I never ask him. We don't ask each other those things. I mean sometimes I'll say to Bernie, can you write a song about so and so, and maybe he will. But it's very rare that I come up with a suggestion for the lyrical content of the song. I don't like treading on his toes, because I know that I'll always like what he comes up with. He's an excellent lyric writer and he's never been given enough credit.

When Elton dropped the last verse to Daniel*, did you feel the sense had been lost?*

BT You know of all the songs that are ever talked about, *Daniel* seems to be the one that always crops up. *Daniel* has been the most misinterpreted song that we've ever written. It's been interpreted as a gay anthem, a family feud song, there's no end to it. I don't know if that last verse had been included, it would have made the song any more understandable. But just to clear it up, the song was inspired by an article that I read when we were recording *Don't Shoot Me* in Chateau d'Arraville outside Paris. I was reading *Newsweek* in bed, late at night, and there was a piece about the vets coming home from Vietnam. The story was about a guy that went back to a small town in Texas. He'd been crippled in the Tet offensive. They'd lauded him when he came home and treated him like a hero. They just wouldn't leave him alone, they insisted that he be a hero, but he just wanted to go home, go back to the farm, and try to get back to the life that he'd led before. I just embellished that and like everything I write, I probably ended up being very esoteric. But it is a song that is important to me, because it was the one thing I said about the Vietnam war. I arrived in this country, at the time that it was going on, and I was here when it was over. But when I give things to Elton, it's very important that I don't lay a big message or my innermost feeling on him, because I'm putting words in to his mouth. In some ways I have to hide it a little, maybe in *Daniel*, I hid it too much. But I wanted to write something that was sympathetic to the people that came home. My idea was of a man wanting to get away from here, to disappear, and it was supposedly sung by his brother, who saw him leave. But hey, it's a song, and it should be inter-preted like any song, the way you want to interpret it.

Daniel

Daniel is travelling tonight on a plane,
I can see the red tail lights heading for Spain,
Oh and I can see Daniel waving goodbye,
God it looks like Daniel, must be the clouds in my eyes.

They say Spain is pretty, though I've never been,
Well, Daniel says it's the best place he's ever seen,
Oh and he should know he's been there enough,
Lord I miss Daniel, Oh I miss him so much.

Oh Daniel my brother,
You are older than me,
Do you still feel the pain
Of the scars that won't heal?
Your eyes have died, but you see more than I,
Daniel you're a star in the face of the sky.

When you and Elton stopped living together, how did you get your lyrics to one another?

BT I moved out of the apartment in Northwood Hills to a cottage in Lincolnshire which I lived in for about a year or so. I was constantly in town so we were seeing each other a lot. We were always in the same location when we worked and then when I moved to the States we would usually be in the same location prior to recording. So the thing about Elton getting my lyrics by mail is something of a fallacy. When we first started writing songs, in the late 60s, I would go back up to Lincolnshire and spend a lot of time up there. So I would probably send some things down by mail, because our volume was much greater when we were working purely as songwriters. When Elton became Elton he was the artist so we were only writing and recording when those records were to be made. We did write a song on the phone once, which is *Don't Go Breaking My Heart*, and it sounds like it was written on the phone.

1971

All The Nasties on the Madman Across The Water album appeared to be directed at the critics. Were you particularly affected by criticism at this time?

EJ I was very sensitive to criticism. After being the darling boy of the radio and critics for the first two years of our career, things took a turn. I now understand that that's a natural process, but I always wanted everything to be wonderful and of course it isn't. I've given up reading the critics. I don't read music papers anymore, I've outgrown them. They're for new bands, they're for the Happy Mondays of the world.

How did you come to write Rocket Man?

BT I'd gone back to my parents' house when they were still living in the north of England, and I remember I was driving down the road, and all of a sudden it was just bang, the whole first verse came into my head – just reeled off, you know; "She packed my bags last night, preflight, zero hour, 9 am, gonna be high as a kite by then". It all came out just like that. And I thought God, I've got to remember that. I drove along at 90 miles an hour, rushed into the house, and started writing it down furiously before I forgot it.

Isn't there a legendary 25 minute version of Rocket Man?

EJ Which I have in my safe keeping. I did it in Melbourne, Australia, when I got absolutely legless doing a television show. I must have had half a bottle of whisky at least, and I did this whole thing about the Ayatollah Khomeini in the middle of it, and the Pope – I mean where I was coming from I do not know. It's an all time winner, that one.

Who was I'm Going To Be A Teenage Idol written about?

EJ Marc Bolan was the inspiration behind it. Bernie

I'm going to be a TEENAGE IDOL

Goodbye Yellowbrick Road *is now viewed as a landmark album – didn't you record some of it in Jamaica?*

EJ How it ever came out like that I'll never know. We'd done *Honky Chateau*, and *Don't Shoot Me* in France, so we thought let's go somewhere else. Well, the Rolling Stones had just done *Goatshead Soup* in Jamaica so we thought let's go there. It's fabulous Jamaica, wonderful. The band went too because we had nothing written. I was too afraid to go out of the hotel room because it was you know – pretty funky, downtown Kingston, and most of those songs were written in two or three days in my hotel room, on an electric piano.

Byron Leigh who had a studio also had a record company – it was like a record plant, and some of the people were picketing, they were on strike. We used to go into the studio in the Volkswagen bus everyday and all these pickets would blow through a blow pipe, and half an hour later we'd all come out in rashes. It was crushed fibreglass they were blowing on us, and we came out in all these blotches.

When we actually got into the studio, the only thing that was ever recorded was a version of *Saturday Night's Alright For Fighting* because when we came back to listen to it in the control room, it sounded as if it had been recorded on the worst transistor radio. We panicked, you know, because at this time we still had budgets to keep to. We'd come all the way here at great expense, all the equipment's here, what are we gonna do? Go back to the Chateau, that was it. Then the nightmare started, they impounded our equipment. During the taxi ride to the airport, the taxi driver took us right through the sugar cane field, I thought I was gonna be killed.

The only great thing about Kingston was the record shacks by the side of the road which were wonderful. But I mean, I'd never seen poverty

and I were very friendly with Marc, and Marc for me was one of the best innovative writers and performers. He wasn't the most brilliant musician, but you don't have to be the most brilliant musician or singer, to get a point across. Marc was a larger than life figure – always happy, seemed to be anyway, he used to come out and say I've sold a million records, he lived in this fantasy land but he was sweet, and loveable, and very, very clever. I still think his records sound tremendous.

before that, I mean I've seen poverty, but never like that. It was just not a good environment to write in. We went straight back to the Chateau and the album was done.

Saturday Night's Alright For Fighting ended up being one of the classic songs on that album.

EJ *Saturday Night* was so hard to record. It's not a typical piano number and in the end the band played it first and I put the piano on afterwards. It was the first song I'd ever done standing up, I actually sang the number just leaping around the studio going crazy.

The single Philadelphia Freedom *was written for Billie Jean King wasn't it?*

EJ There have been isolated incidents where we've written singles as a one-off thing. *Philadelphia Freedom* was one, *Don't Go Breaking My Heart* was another. It worked with *Philadelphia*, it was the right time, the right place, and the right sound of music. Philadelphia was coming up with some great music, the OJ's, The Three Degrees, Billy Paul, and all that. But it was a tribute to the Tennis Team. I wanted to write something for Billie Jean as she was such a great influence on me as a person. I really loved her energy and I loved her forthright views on everything. She's remained a good friend all that time up to the present day and it's still one of my favourite songs.

How did you come to write Philadelphia Freedom?

BT The reason I wrote that was purely because Elton wanted me to write it. He was playing tennis with Billie Jean King at the time and she had a tennis team called the Philadelphia Freedoms. Also the music coming out of Philadelphia was real predominant in the charts and Elton was a big, big fan of all that stuff. He asked me to write something

Elton with Billie Jean King 1975

60

and I came up with *Philadelphia Freedom*. I think I had a little difficulty with it but I must admit I don't remember actually how I came up with a synopsis of the song. It's an esoteric song about feeling free.

---

*"*I was going to a concert in a limo with Elton, and he says: "I'm gonna write a song for you, would you like that?" I said, "Are you kidding? That would be great". At that time with world team tennis he was like our mascot. He used to wear the track suit and come and sit on the bench with us. Anyway, he says, "I'm gonna talk to Bernie and have him write some lyrics and we're gonna call it after you". And sure enough in Denver with the Philadelphia tennis team he had all of us listen to the rough mix of *Philadelphia Freedom.* He was so nervous that I wasn't gonna like it, but I loved it because it has that Philadelphia sound that I really do like. It's just so thoughtful that they wrote a song and dedicated it to me. It meant a lot.*"*

Billy Jean King

Many people would say that Captain Fantastic *was your finest album. Do you agree?*

EJ Yeah, it's one of the best. One of the hardest things about making an album is that you have to put a running order together and it takes quite a long time. *Captain Fantastic* was written in sequence, as it was an autobiographical album, so it was easier to write in that respect. I'd love to do that again, have the running order first, because then you can control the sound of the record. I think it was a very, very good album musically and production wise it was probably one of the finest albums.

Do you remember where you wrote that?

EJ I wrote some of it on the S.S. France, going from Southampton to New York, and some of it in the studio. It was written over a period – because I had all the lyrics in advance, it was a totally different sort of album, it was an isolated case as far as lyrics go.

At that time of Blue Moves *Elton says he found all the lyrics were downbeat. Did he ever reject any lyrics you sent him at that time?*

BT It's not rejection, it's just what works best. Whenever we write an album we overwrite. If there are 12 songs on an album, we'll write 15 or 16 and I'll write 20 pieces so there may be five that he tries to work on that he can't get into, and the rest he'll write and we'll pick out the best. Some of them we'll record and reject, some of them won't even get recorded. I think Elton had a lot of difficulty with *Blue Moves* because it was a blue period for both of us. I like to think that the things we write include both of us but it's difficult at times because he doesn't live the same life as me. I know Elton well enough to put myself in his head and to know his feelings at certain times, but *Blue Moves* was probably a little self indulgent, because it was very much what I was going through at the time. I think I sank too much into depressive excess on that album. When you start writing songs about someone's final song, about suicidal writers blowing their brains out, about Edith Piaf and stuff like that, it makes it a very depressive album. There were a lot of really dark songs but that's me, I like darkness, I can't help it – that's where a lot of it comes from, you know.

1972

Elton with Cher, 1973

"Elton and I were going to the Paul McCartney concert together. I was really nervous, because I was pregnant, and I don't like crowds to begin with, it was really difficult. And then on the way home he was saying that he wanted to apologise, it wasn't his fault. And I said it wasn't your fault for what? He said well, for the song. And I said what song? He said well on the back of *Don't Go Breaking My Heart*, Bernie wrote this terrible song about you called *Snow Queen*, he said Bernie was really furious with you and you know what, I've never heard it, but I know it's real nasty."

Cher

Does it feel odd singing a song for someone else?

EJ No, it never has done actually. That's another thing that's quite extraordinary. The album that I identify most with would be *Captain Fantastic*, because it was about the two of us. But songs like *Blue Moves*, there's a lot of pain in those songs, because Bernie was going through some really bad personal stuff at the time. So I've been the man who sang the pain. But I never look at the lyrics and say I can't sing this. I get the first line of a song or the title, and I work from there. You know sometimes I'm not really aware of what the song's about until I've written it. It's an oddball way to write songs, and I haven't really given it much deep thought, but I don't see why we should change it.

"I don't think I could handle expressing someone else's lyrics. I'll sit down with the guitar, and just let the unconscious start to work, say whatever comes into my head, then pursue that and try to make a verse out of it. Elton's approach is much more classical. He attended the Royal Academy, so that gives him an immediate slant on music. If I heard a Tamla record, I was listening to the guitar and the drums, perhaps Elton was listening to the chord structures and the composition. Composition came very late into my life as an interesting theory, and probably Elton had that in his mind all the time, which is why songwriting comes so easily to him."

Eric Clapton

Do you think that people believe that what you're singing about is what you feel?

EJ I think so, I hope so. Because when you do a vocal in the studio, you put your soul into it. There are various things that I wish I could redo in the studio. The *Madman Across The Water* album has some vocals that I would like to redo again. I'm not afraid now when the red light goes on in the studio, but in those days I was petrified. Everything I've done in the studio I've done with the passion that I thought it should have. And sometimes it comes over and sometimes it doesn't. Sometimes when you write a song the demo is better than the actual track that you record. That's why I try not to do demos anymore. Occasionally, after you do the demo, you go in to record the thing and it just hasn't got the atmosphere, and the atmosphere is so essential to a song and to the sound of the record. If you hear a record and it grasps you within ten seconds, you know that song's gonna do well. Prime examples of that are *I'm Not in Love* – 10CC, *Radio Gaga* – Queen, *Nothing Compares 2 U* – Sinead O'Connor – just the intros and the atmosphere created. It doesn't happen all that often, but when it does, it's magic.

How did you feel when Bernie used your experiences as in Someone Saved My Life Tonight?

EJ It was nice to be able to sing about me for once, about one of my experiences, because I've always been singing about his ideas and his experiences. It was a very personal album, so it's very dear to me. *We All Fall in Love* and *Curtains* still make me cry when I listen to them.

What's the story behind Someone Saved My Life Tonight?

EJ I was going to get married once when I was younger, and I went out and got drunk with Long John Baldry and Bernie, and John said I shouldn't get married. I knew he was right but I didn't know how to get out of it, so I just got drunk and went home and said I'm not getting married. It took a lot of alcohol to make me say it, but I did and if I had got married, it wouldn't have happened for Bernie and me like it did, it's just fate.

BT We were living at the flat in Islington and Elton was destined to tie the knot. He wasn't very sure about it, and he was getting more and more depressed. He talked about ending it all. I was, of course, totally sympathetic and said yeah, right, sure, go ahead, you're all mouth. So one day as I was coming out of my room and walking down the hall, I smelt gas. I thought oh, great, somebody's left the oven on in the kitchen. I walk in the kitchen and there's Elton lying on the floor, with the gas oven open. My immediate thing should have been, oh, my God, he's tried to kill himself. But I started laughing because he'd got the gas oven open, he was lying on a pillow and he'd opened all the windows. So it wasn't as desperate as I thought. I dragged him out of there and I remember running into the bedroom where

Someone Saved My Life Tonight

When I think of those East End lights
Muggy nights,
The curtains drawn in the little room downstairs.
Prima Donna lord you really should have been there,
Sitting like a princess perched in her electric chair.
And it's one more beer,
And I don't hear you anymore.
We've all gone crazy lately,
My friend's out there rolling round the basement floor.

And someone saved my life tonight, sugar bear,
You almost had your hooks in me didn't you dear,
You nearly had me roped and tied,
Altar-bound, hypnotised.
Sweet freedom whispered in my ear
You're a butterfly,
And butterflies are free to fly
Fly away, high away bye bye.

I never realised the passing hours
Of evening showers,
A slip noose hanging in my darkest dreams,
I'm strangled by your haunted social scene
Just a pawn out-played by a dominating queen
It's four-o-clock in the morning
Damn it!
Listen to me good,
I'm sleeping with myself tonight
Saved in time, thank God my music's still alive.

And I would have walked head on into the deep end of a river,
Clinging to your stocks and bonds
Paying your H.P. demands forever.
They're coming in the morning with a truck to take me home.
Someone saved my life tonight, someone saved my life tonight.
Someone saved my life tonight, someone saved my life tonight.
Someone saved my life tonight.
So save your strength and run the field you play alone.

his fiancée was, saying "Quick, quick, Elton's tried to commit suicide, I need help". I remember his fiancée just looking at me. She was watching television and eating something, she looked at me and said "Oh, not again," or words to that effect, "he'll be alright". A totally sympathetic answer, I thought. But anyway, it was a pretty unique attempt.

But it inspired a song – Someone Saved My Life Tonight?

BT When I wrote *Someone Saved My Life Tonight*, it was not necessarily about that suicide attempt, it was about his being saved from getting married which would have been a disaster at that time. Just saving himself from himself, and inspiring him. I think people around him inspired him to a new level. So that song, like a lot of songs, incorporates a lot of different aspects; the love of family, the love of friends, the whole thing.

One of your biggest hits was Your Song. *How do you feel about it now?*

BT I guess if anybody's going to use the word standard in our repertoire, *Your Song* is going to be it. I always had this kind of battle with *Your Song*, sometimes I hate it, and sometimes I love it. You always dislike the songs that you hear the most and you hear that one everywhere, you go in Safeway you hear it, in the elevator in the Holiday Inn. You hear it in the Piano Bar at a Holiday Inn, you hear it all over the Holiday Inn. It's become a Holiday Inn song. So you tend to lose respect for it. But then there are times when I'll be at one of Elton's shows, and the spotlight will hit, and Elton'll do that song, and it'll take on a whole new meaning, it'll drag me all the way back to when I was sixteen, when I wrote it. And it sounds like a sixteen-year-old wrote it. It sounds like a song that was written by a guy that never got laid in his life,

which I hadn't at that point. There's a story about Elton swearing blind that I wrote it about this girl I was going out with at the time, but I swear blind that I didn't. I do remember that I wrote it during breakfast at the flat in Northwood Hills, it was just something that came off the top of my head. There's nothing mesmerising about the way I wrote it, I was eating scrambled eggs and writing at the same time – there's a legend killer if ever there was one. But it's a great song. The songs of ours that I like tend to be the ones that you don't hear very much. I never get tired of hearing *Candle in the Wind*. There are some of our songs that are the perfect mesh of lyric and melody and I think *Candle in the Wind* is one of them. The only

thing that bothers me about the song is that as a result people tend to think that I have a raging obsession with Marilyn Monroe which was not the point of the song. The point of the song was how the media distorts people's lives. It's a bit like *Daniel*, people are not left alone, and that's really

Candle In The Wind

> *Goodbye Norma Jean*
> *Though I never knew you at all*
> *You had the grace to hold yourself*
> *While those around you crawled*
> *They crawled out of the woodwork*
> *And they whispered into your brain*
> *They set you on the treadmill*
> *And they made you change your name.*

>> *And it seems to me you lived your life*
>> *Like a candle in the wind*
>> *Never knowing who to cling to*
>> *When the rain set in*
>> *And I would have liked to have known you*
>> *But I was just a kid*
>> *Your candle burned out long before*
>> *Your legend ever did.*

>> *Loneliness was tough*
>> *The toughest role you ever played*
>> *Hollywood created a superstar*
>> *And the pain was the price you paid*
>> *Even when you died*
>> *The press still hounded you*
>> *All the papers had to say*
>> *Was that Marilyn was found in the nude.*

>>> *Goodbye Norma Jean*
>>> *Though I never knew you at all*
>>> *You had the grace to hold yourself*
>>> *While those around you crawled.*

>>> *Goodbye Norma Jean*
>>> *From the young man in the 22nd row*
>>> *Who sees you as something more than sexual*
>>> *More than just our Marilyn Monroe.*

what *Candle in the Wind* was about. It's a song about media abuse. How we abuse the living, how we abuse the dead. I'm not saying she wasn't talented, but sometimes it pays to die – that's what that song's about.

Did Bernie talk to you about his ideas for example, when he was thinking of Candle in the Wind?

EJ We never communicate like that. He goes away, writes, gives it to me, and that's the end of it, there's no other process. At one stage, I thought my albums were sounding disjointed. The *Reg Strikes Back* album, for example, had so many different sorts of music it didn't gel for me, so on *Sleeping With The Past* we really wanted to make an effort to gel all the songs together, and we did that. We came up with the idea of writing soul-type lyrics, all one feel of lyrics, which we've never really done before. *Sleeping With The Past* was the last album I made, and that was the end of a twenty-year era of making records for me. I really love that album a lot but I don't want to go back and make that sort of album again. I don't know what direction my music's gonna take. I have no fear of writing, I know I can always write. I just really hate the business at the moment, the videos and all that. I'm not part of that, I've never felt comfortable with it. Sometimes it works. *I'm Still Standing* was a really nice video, and *Nikita* was a good video, *Sacrifice* was a well-made video. But I don't feel like a video artist, and I resent the fact that I have to do a video to publicise a song. A song should stand or fall on its own merit.

Bernie's got very into making videos. He was in Passengers *and helped with* Healing Hands. *Has he suggested ideas to you?*

EJ He gets together with video directors in Los Angeles a lot of the time. I like to get him involved in projects because I want him to be a part of it. Because he's the lyric writer he knows what should be portrayed visually more than I do so I think it's very important to include him.

You led the way a lot with Sleeping With The Past *didn't you?*

BT From 1967 through to the mid-seventies, there was a very definite way that we worked. I wrote, gave it to him, he wrote, bang, bang, bang, and there's your song. But later I became more musically orientated and more in tune with him, and less afraid of approaching him with my ideas. We made a pact before we did *Sleeping With The Past*. We decided that whatever we wrote we would get together and talk about. So, there was a preconceived idea about what we were going to write. The songs were to be based upon great songs, songs that we grew up with, or that were R & B classics. It's a white-black album, written by two white kids from England. I would say to Elton, this is my idea for a Ray Charles-type song, this is my idea of a Sam and Dave song, this is my idea of Ben E. King, and so on.

Why did you dedicate Sleeping With The Past *to Bernie?*

EJ It was an important album for us. *Reg Strikes Back* had been made because I went back to work after being intensely unhappy. I had three years of my life that were really unhappy, personal things going wrong and stuff like that. *Reg Strikes Back* was mostly to get me back in the studio, it had two or three really nice things on it. But when you're an artist you know that you can't afford to come out with mediocre stuff all the time, and there were songs on there that I didn't really like. But it served a purpose, it got me back, got me out of the house. With *Sleeping* we just wanted every song on it to be great, and Bernie worked really hard to come up with the same sort of lyrics, so that I could have a theme running through the album. He was sort of living in England when he was writing those songs and we spent a lot of time together, not writing, but we spent a lot of time together, and I really wanted to say how valuable our relationship was and how much I admired and respected him. I wanted just to express that I actually think the world of him, I didn't tell him in advance I was gonna do it.

BT I was very, very touched. I think he dedicated it to me because he felt that in *Sleeping With The Past* we found a new unity in our writing. It was the first album where we stripped it all down and really talked about what we do best and the best thing that we do together is write songs, and for the first time he regarded me on a musical level and that meant a great deal to me. He realised that I'd come to that point where I had won my spurs, and he treated me with a great respect on that album. Hopefully I gave it back to him.

Do the songs tell a story when you look back on the body of work? Can you tell when you're unhappy?

EJ I knew when I was unhappy. I knew when he was unhappy. There were lots of happy times and lots of bad times, people go through that all the time. We're no different because we're famous. The bad times were mostly self-inflicted. It got to the point where in the end I didn't really appreciate anything that I had left. I was really worn out, and I needed to take some time away from my career and get my life personally back together.

'Sleeping With The Past was the first album where we stripped it all down and really talked about what we do best — and the best thing we do together is to write songs'

SKYLINE PIGEON.   DWIGHT/TAUPIN
Eb.

TURN ME LOOSE FROM YOUR HANDS
LET ME FLY TO DISTANT LANDS,
OVER GREEN FIELDS TREES AND MOUNTAINS
FLOWERS AND FOREST FOUNTAINS
HOME ALONG THE LANES OF THE SKYWAY.

FOR THIS DARKENED LONELY ROOM
PROJECTS A SHADOW CAST IN GLOOM.
AND MY EYES ARE MIRRORS OF THE WORLD OUTSIDE
THINKING OF THE WAYS THAT THE WIND CAN TURN THE TIDE
AND THESE SHADOWS TURN FROM PURPLE INTO GREY.

FOR JUST THIS SKYLINE PIGEON, DREAMING OF THE OPEN
WAITING FOR THE DAY, THAT HE MAY SPREAD HIS WINGS AND
FLY AWAY AGAIN

FLY AWAY, SKYLINE PIGEON, FLY
TOWARDS THE THINGS YOU'VE LEFT SO VERY FAR BEHIND,

JUST LET ME WAKE UP IN THE MORNING TO THE SMELL OF NEW MOWN
HAY
TO LAUGH AND CRY TO LIVE AND DIE, IN THE BRIGHTNESS OF MY
DAY.
Sun.

I WANT TO HEAR THE PEELING BELLS OF DISTANT CHURCHES
BUT MOST OF ALL PLEASE FREE ME FROM THIS ACHING METAL RING
AND OPEN OUT THIS CAGE TOWARDS THE SUN.

FOR JUST THIS SKYLINE PIGEON, DREAMING OF THE OPEN,
WAITING FOR THE DAY, THAT HE MAY SPREAD HIS WINGS AND FLY
AWAY

FLY AWAY, SKYLINE PIGEON, FLY
TOWARDS THE YOU LEFT SO VERY FAR BEHIND.

REPEAT.

I'm Still Standing

You could never know what it's like

Your blood like winter freezes just like ice

And there's a cold and lonely light that shines from you

You'll wind up like the wreck you hide

Behind that mask you use

did you think this fool could never win

Well look at me, I'm the one comin' back again

I got a taste of love in a simple way

And if you need to know, while I'm still standing

You just fade away

And don't you know, that I'm still standing

Better than I ever did

Lookin' like a true survivor

Feelin' like a little kid

And I'm still standing

After all this time

Pickin' up the pieces of my life

Without you on my mind

Once I could never hope to win

You starting down the road, leaving me again

The threats you made were only meant to cut me down

And if our love was just a circus
You'd BE A CLOWN BY NOW
There's a clown inside you now

Taupin. 9.82

TO LOW FOR ZERO.

SIX-O-CLOCK ALARM, I GET THE WAKE UP CALL
LET THAT SUCKER JINGLE-JANGLE, RING RIGHT O
IM TO LOW FOR ZERO, IM TO TIRED TO WORK.
TIED ONE ON WITH A FRIEND LAST NIGHT
WOUND UP LOOSING MY SHIRT.

IM TO LOW FOR ZERO, IM ON A LOOSING STREAK
IN GOT MYSELF IN A BAD PATCH LATELY
CANT SEEM TO GET MUCH SLEEP
IM TO LOW FOR ZERO, I WIND UP COUNTING SHEEP
NOTHING SEEMS TO MAKE MUCH SENSE
ALL JUST GREEK TO ME.

TO LOW, IM TO LOW, IM TO LOW FOR ZERO
TO LOW, IM TO LOW, IM TO LOW FOR ZERO

OUT CUPS OF COFFEE, SWITCHIN' OF THE LATE NIGHT NEWS
THE CAT OUT TWO HOURS EARLY, ISNT ANY USE
LOW FOR ZERO, INSOMNIA ATTACKS
FLIES WITH MY EYES TILL SUNRISE
IGHT WHEN I HIT THE SACK.

HELP, MAYBE SOM

---

lady Samantha

The railings ring if years over the river
the song winds where silent as ice in the
and must sweep around as a cloak for the winter
and all around waifs of Autumn came tumbling ground
down
then when shrill winds are screaming and
evening is still
lady Samantha glides over the hills
in a long satin dress that she wears everyday
her home is the hillside, her bed is the grave
-
lady Samantha glides like a tiger
over the hills with no one beside her
no wolf comes near, they all live in fear
and lady Samantha sheds only tears
-
the tales that are told round the fire every night
are out of proportion and none of them right
she is harmless and empty of anything bad
see once had something that most of you have

Repeat 2.3.

BJTaupin

Queen

Weary days
the rooms
your childr
and left y
But just i
what happen
one of the
the other
But your l
and your h
for your e
is complet

There's on
lonely and
maybe a le
to help he
She's the
ruler of t
no one com
the queen

Under the
thinking
and went
Your phot
they are
but now t
with plen
without t

There's on
lonely and
maybe a le
to help he
She's the
ruler of
no one com
the queen
the queen
the queen
Oh yes sh
ruler of
no one co
queen of

Scarecrow.

Ⓐ

Your to low to see me smiling
when Im flying in the air,
but your to high to frighten me.
Pretend you did'nt see me
pretend you did'nt need me To frighten away
to frighten away
all the lost and the lonely
the sacred forgotten of yesterdays problems.
Your wooden construction
was meant for infliction
to penetrate pain
with the thoughts from my mind.

Can you see me scarecrow?
can you still feel free,
for are'nt you a scarecrow
and will you still be there tommorrow.

Like moths round a light bulb
your brain is still bleeding
from visions and pictures of natures
young raincoat.
If only my eyes
where not pinned to your table
my arms would be grasping
the lilac of summer.
Its no good to me a scarecrow cant see,
I've said it before
and Ill say it some more.
Can you see me scarecrow?
can you still feel free,
for are'nt you a scarecrow
and will you still be there tommorrow.
Scarecrow

     scarecrow

          scarecrow

               scarecrow.

Ⓞ

Hey Nikita is it cold
in your little corner of the world
you could roll around the globe
and never find a warmer soul to know

I saw you by the wall
ten of your tin soldiers in a row
with your eyes that looked like ice on fire
your heart's like a blood red rose in the snow
Oh Nikita you'll never no anything about
                              My home.
And Ill never know how good it feels to
                        hold you.
Oh Nikita the otherside of any given line
                              in time

First one of ten tin soldiers in a row
Oh no no Nikita, Nikita you'll
          never know

EMPTY GARDEN (HEY HEY JOHNNY)
SPITEFUL CHILD / SLICE OF LIFE
WHERE HAVE ALL THE GOOD TIMES GONE
ROBOT MAN (I AM YOUR)
THE ACE OF HEARTS AND THE JACK OF SPADES.
WAKING UP IN EUROPE
JERRYS LAW
IM NOT VERY WELL
THE DESPERATION TRAIN

THINKING OF LIFE IN EUROPE.
MORAL MAJORITY
IM NOT VERY WELL
QUIET ON THE WESTERN FRONT.

Ballad of a well known gun.

I pulled out my stage coach times
and read the latest news
I tapped my feet in dumb surprise
and of course I saw they new

The Pinkertons pulled out my bags
and asked me for my name
I stuttered out my answers
and hung my head in shame

now they found me
at last they found me
its hard to run
in a starving family
oh now they found me
well I wont run
cause Im tired of hearing
there goes a well known gun

Now I've seen the old chain gang
please let me see my priest
I couldn't have faced your desert sand
old burning brown backed beast.

Now the poorhouse hit me for my keep
and chained my crumbling walls
now I know how Reno felt
when he ran from the law.

TOURING

'People who have hit records come and go, but you can't sustain a career unless you can play live'

Do you think you learned a lot in the years you were trudging around the clubs?

EJ I think the vital thing in my career has been playing live, I mean one can make records that go up and down the charts. But to sustain a career, I think you really have to be a good live musician. And the years that I spent as a youth, trudging up and down the countryside with Bluesology, backing people like Patti LaBelle, Major Lance, and Billy Stewart, did me a world of good, because when you're young and you're in the back of a van, even though it's uncomfortable and you're all pooling your money for your gasoline or your petrol, you feel happy at being able to do what you've always dreamed of doing. The finances don't really enter into it, you just muddle through somehow. There were times when we worked extremely hard, two or three shows a day sometimes. And then we were with Long John Baldry, who was an English blues legend. He was a lovely man to work for, and a big influence on me, just as a person. He was very kind to his musicians, he always saw to them first, I respected him for that. When I actually came to doing live shows as Elton John, it was invaluable all that groundwork, all that solid base.

People who have hit records come and go, but you can't sustain a career unless you can play live. And I don't mean just lip-synching or playing to a drum track because that's not playing live. A lot of artists go out there and do that nowadays and that's why they have the charisma of a dead pea. When I go to concerts and hear that it's a drum machine, and it's all pre-recorded, it goes for me. Some of the public can't tell, but I think in the end, they can, they like to see people make mistakes on stage, to see people actually learning their craft and playing instruments.

Nowadays people get signed up, make a record, and then swan around if it's a hit. But when they go on tour they haven't got the experience and the knowledge to do a 45 minute set, it's all new to them. To anybody that's starting off, I would say, go and play, it doesn't matter where it is, how small it is, just go and play, learn the craft and enjoy those first few years of your life, when you're able to go on the road. From 1970 to '74, when I went on the road as Elton John we played so many tours, made so many albums, and we never considered it hard work, it was wonderful to be able to do what we did; meeting new people, playing with people that we idolised. Then I became really famous, and things changed a little after that.

> "I first saw Elton when he was Reg with Bluesology at the Marquee. There were three singers and he was in the backing band. I remember him even then. I remember what he looked like and his playing. A couple of years later he was Elton John. We obviously came into contact a lot at different functions. We had a lot of mutual friends. I think the first time I really started to get to know him was as late as '85 with the Prince's Trust. And I've since grown to love him very much, I think he's a great guy, really lovely."
>
> *Phil Collins*

What did Bernie do when you were on tour?

EJ Most of the time, in the early days he came with us, he was part of the family, he was part of the team. It would have been unthinkable not to have

Elton in Bluesology

Bernie with us. He still comes on every tour that I do at some point. But there's only so many times you can see *Funeral for a Friend*, and *Loves Lies Bleeding* without going stark raving mad, so I understand why he stays at home sometimes.

We've got film of one of your first TV appearances in concert, with the BBC 1970. You used that show to introduce Bernie, was that unusual?

EJ He was very much a partner in everything I did, and when he came on live shows with us on tour I always used to try and put him on stage at the end and say this is Bernie, because his lyrics mean an awful lot to a lot of people. He was very shy and reticent about going on stage but I always made him come out. It was nice to credit him. It was important for him and for me, because I didn't think he was getting enough credit. I mean without Bernie, there were no songs.

BT It was the first BBC live broadcast. I don't remember being introduced. I was probably thoroughly embarrassed. I'm not really crazy on media attention now, so you can imagine how I felt back then.

Tell me about your first American gig at The Troubadour, Los Angeles

EJ The way to sell records in those days was by doing live shows. A lot of bands who were very, very popular in this country, like Geno Washington and the Ram Jam Band, took a long time to get a recording contract. Things were done the other way in those days, you went out on the road and sold records for a following. So when my records didn't sell that well, I had to go back on the road, which was something I didn't want to do, it was like fate really. I got Nigel Olsson and Dee Murray together, and we went out as a three piece band. And everything really catapulted when we went

to America and played that first night at the Troubadour club. That was the first time I knew something really big was happening, that was really when I became Elton, I mean I was Elton before that, but that was when I really launched into Elton John. The review from Robert Hilburn, in *The Los Angeles Times*, made us stars in the main cities in America before we even played them. Word of mouth spread very, very quickly, this is the new person, this is it, this is the new big thing. Ironically, I didn't wanna go to Los Angeles and play the Troubadour club at that time, I really wanted to stay in England and get a following playing live here. We went really under duress, which seems strange now when I look back on it. I didn't think the timing was right, and Dick James said the timing was right, and Dick James was absolutely correct. It all happened, exploded from that point on – I really mean exploded.

What do you remember of the Troubadour gig in LA that night?

BT That was like the first or second day we were here, so I was still mesmerised by my surroundings. I don't really remember much about it. It didn't hit us till a few days later, because we didn't know what kind of impact we'd made. It was just, God, we get to play in America, we get to buy records in America, get to go to Tower Records, great looking girls. It was fabulous – it was the candy store. It's still like that to me. I go all over the world and I come back here and everything's fabulous. At the Troubadour the people that turned up and saw us were amazing. I can only imagine how Elton must have felt because he was playing in front of them. He had Leon Russell in the front row. I remember Elton saying God, Leon Russell's gonna take me away and tie me up and say "Hey kid, this is how you play the piano".

I was always nervous when Elton played, I mean I lived vicariously through him going on stage; because he didn't have any paranoia I had it all for him.

> "The Troubadour was sensational. The turnout was something we couldn't have imagined. Russ Reagan and the record company had done a very good job, hyping the event. At the time Elton's big favourite was Leon Russell. He totally freaked when he saw Leon Russell sitting in the front row. We were all overawed with the whole thing. But he put on the most incredible show and you knew that night, that a star was born."
>
> *Ray Williams*

How did you and Bernie feel when Dylan came to visit you?

EJ We played the Fillmore East in New York, with Leon Russell who was my idol at that time and Dylan was at the gig. I don't think he came to see us. I think he was there with Leon. But I remember he sort of mentioned something about

us. I didn't really remember much because I was so in awe of Dylan being there, and Bernie was like a nervous wreck. We were still excited in those early days by meeting people, we played with the Byrds, we played with Poco, we played with people that we'd bought records of, and it happened so quickly. George Harrison sent me a telegram saying congratulations. I mean this is someone who'd gone from making an album to being kind of a star, very, very quickly. But thank God I was prepared for that; we were a live act and we could just go out and play. We did a lot of live work in America and the rest of the world for five years.

BT The high point of the first couple of tours we did was Dylan coming to the Fillmore. Elton came back to the dressing room, and said there's somebody I want you to meet, and he dragged me over. I didn't even recognise him. Elton said this is Bob Dylan, I wasn't really ready for it, what can I say? I mean it was like, oh God, or you're God, or my God.

> "They went to see Bob Dylan, on the Isle of Wight, and I remember getting a postcard saying, we've been to see God."
>
> *Bernie's Mum*

You're friends now?

BT Oh I wouldn't say that, I mean we're acquaintances. In this business when people say they've spent time together, time together is like five minutes in a room, or a dressing room somewhere. It's certainly a different situation than it was back then, I can walk into a room with him and not collapse in a babbling wreck on the floor. I can sit down and talk about basketball with him.

Dodgers Stadium 1975

Some of those early tours were like family outings. Do you remember Dodger Stadium?

EJ It wasn't a happy period of my life, but they were great shows. After the *Blue Moves* tour, I really needed a break. I'd worked solidly for six years and you can get fed up with the sound of your own voice and the sound of the songs. Certain songs you sing for a long period of time, and you have to drop them because you can't face singing them again for a while. *Your Song*, I must have sung in 90% of the shows I've done, but there are times when I can't face singing it.

Is it a vivid image, Dodger Stadium, even now?

EJ Not really, I remember Cary Grant being there, I remember crying – coming off stage. It was a very big show for us to do. Not many people did outside shows in those days and we did two days there, we pulled it off, you have to pull off the big events, and we usually did. All my family was there, we flew everyone on an aircraft over from England; it had to be good. You have to have that ability as a performer to pull those ones off; on every tour you do you need one big one at least, so that your adrenalin still flows. Because other-wise it can be a bit run of the mill.

> "Dodger Stadium was unbelievable. It was great to walk out and see all the candles and people dancing in the field. It was one of the best nights of my life, seeing 65,000 people swaying back and forth to the music and being totally involved in the moment."
>
> Billie Jean King

Did Bernie ever get annoyed with your antics on stage?

EJ Yeah, very. Bernie hated some of the costumes that I wore, hated some of the things that I did, but I had to be me. I think I took it too far in retrospect, but I can't regret that now. He was embarrassed by some of it, and he will admit that freely. And looking back on some of the pictures, I can see why. But he's never said listen if you don't stop wearing those things, I won't come to the show. There's never been that power thing between the two of us. Unfortunately the more people said to me you can't do things, the more I did them. I was just having fun to start with. And even after it stopped being fun, for a while I had to carry on that image, even though I didn't feel comfortable about it. There have been things that I regret but after twenty years of still being in the top echelon of artists and songwriters, the things I regret most are personal things.

BT Seeing Elton deliver something like *Your Song* or *Border Song* with Mickey Mouse ears or a Donald Duck outfit has never been one of my favourite things in life, but underneath he's the only person that could do that and still make it sound worthwhile. Elton knows that I never felt any of that was necessary but then I could be totally wrong and had it not been for the theatrics and the costumes, the glasses and the boots and the feathers and the colours, it wouldn't have gained the attention it did, and through that the attention to the songs. But the core of it is the songs and the core of it will always be the songs. Now that I look back on it I don't regret the plumage and the peacock and the fans and all that. At least he did it before anybody else. I know people like to think of him as the Liberace of Rock but Liberace never had that much soul.

U.S. Tour 1974

Didn't you once dress up as Tina Turner?

EJ Yeah, I've been in drag a couple of times on stage, at Madison Square Garden I came on dressed as Tina Turner, in the same outfit that she wore on the *What's Love Got To Do With It?* video. I didn't

> "He met me backstage at a show in Wembley and we were trying on shoes – and the shoes fitted. The next thing I got was this framed photograph of him in the jean jacket and the leather skirt and high heels. I still have it. It's hung on my wall and everyone thinks it's me and I always have to say it's Elton John. That was too close, Elton."
>
> *Tina Turner*

> "The first concert I went to was at the Forum in Los Angeles and Elton came dressed as Minnie Mouse. That's my big memory of that concert."
>
> *Sting*

> "I couldn't wear the things he wears – I mean it's been said before probably too many times that he's this generation's Liberace but it's him, you know, he manages to wear that stuff and pull it off."
>
> *Phil Collins*

tell anybody that I was going to do it. Not even anybody in the band. There was complete and utter silence as I stalked across the stage in my high heeled shoes and people thought who's that? I sat down and played *Yellow Brick Road*, and then they went, oh Christ. I have a picture of me taken by a fan from the back, my legs aren't bad actually, and I think that was quite funny. I don't give a fuck about that sort of thing. And I went on stage recently with Rod Stewart in drag. I enjoy getting up in drag, it's the pantomime thing. After I've had it on for about 15 minutes I can't wait to get it off, but I don't like to take much of that seriously. Maybe people have said, you spoilt the music by wearing those outfits, and you didn't take the music seriously, but the music stood up for itself. I was just trying to be Reg trying to be Elton, and Elton was trying to be Reg, and it was all going on and it was fun, and it was hell, it was great and it was not great.

What was your favourite tour?

BT There are different moments in different tours. There were the tours of tremendous excess, in the late 70s which probably were fun but I have trouble recalling any of them. There are the tours where the musical content was the most inspiring, and probably one of those was the solo tour to Russia with Ray Cooper. Because the satisfaction of hearing our songs stripped down in their rawest state was very exciting. Fans of ours that have been fans for years always say that that was their favourite tour, which is really heartwarming for me, because that shows that they really care about the songs. The flamboyance is something else, the volume is something else. People tend to think in order to make something exciting you just have to turn up the amps. That's not what it's about. It's about intensity. It's about passion, it's about how you convey the songs. If you go on and you inspire, it beats all the wattage and ampage you can crank up because it's all in the song.

Bernie talked about the tour in Russia, that was very simple, just you and Ray Cooper. Did that make you look at the lyrics again?

EJ Yes. Having just the piano and the percussion player improved my singing and my interpretation of the lyrics. I rediscovered the songs all over again, and realised what great lyrics and songs they were. I don't really stay in the past, which is a good thing, but on the other hand I've sometimes written off what I've done. When people say to me oh, you've made some great songs, I always go oh yeah. But we have written some good songs. It's very important to acknowledge that. When I did the rehearsals for that tour I sang a lot of songs that I hadn't sung on stage for a long time, and I had to concentrate. It was one of the best things I've ever done.

What do you think of his new image?

BT I love his new image. Elton wears it well. Elton's achieved a new plateau in his life. He's happy with himself and if he's happy, then I'm ecstatic. He obviously found something in the last couple of years that he relates to, God bless him, if he's found that kind of contentment then I think together we'll find a new direction because I know that we need a new direction. I know from my own standpoint that I've got to do something different.

Do you think of Elton as a balladier or a rock and roller?

BT Elton is everything. Elton's the consummate performer, the consummate musician. Elton rocks, Elton's soft, Elton plays the best rock 'n' roll piano ever and he can deliver a ballad better than anybody I know, he enjoys it, and that's why he's so good at it. People think the older we get the less we're allowed to rock or kick out or have fun, but look at John Lee Hooker, he still kicks butt and how old is he, 79? It's funny how the older our generation gets the more we're called dinosaurs but the older the guys from the 30s and 40s get, the more they're called legends. I don't understand that. You can rock until they bury you in your grave. If Elton didn't think he was capable of doing it, he wouldn't pretend to.

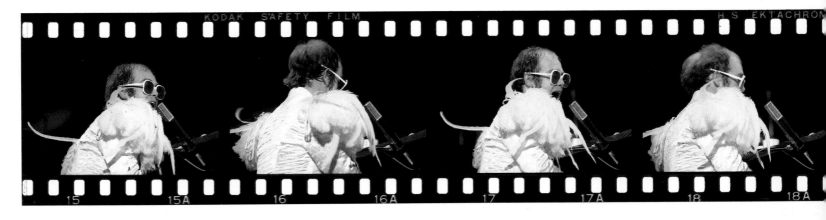

AMERICA

Let's talk about when you came to America for the first time, what were your first thoughts?

BT When I first came to the States, I kissed the ground and said I'm staying here, you ain't getting me back. It was all my childhood dreams come true, everything was bigger, everything was brighter, everything was more vibrant, it was all the things I imagined it would be, I wasn't let down at all. I knew within the first week I was here that I wanted to stay. My spirit belonged here. Only a very few dreams are endearing, and England was a dream that faded out.

Judging by Mona Lisas and Madhatters, *you weren't so enamoured with New York.*

BT No. Again, it's about naiveté and experience. I wrote *Mona Lisas and Madhatters* the day after we first went to New York, and I mean, I'd never been to any place like it – it was unbelievable. I was still very naive, we were both still naive and New York seemed like the bowels of hell. The first day that we got there, somebody was shot outside my hotel. Now, years later, I've experienced New York and there's good sides and bad sides, you know.

With your love of American Soul Music, were you never tempted to move there?

EJ I had a house in Los Angeles for a while as a necessity. I was spending so much time in America that I needed a base, because I'm really a home-loving boy. But I've always liked my base here. America is so fabulous that I like to leave it and go back to get my fix. I love the American people, I love touring America, but I don't know what would have happened if I'd lived there permanently. I always look forward to going to America and that's never dulled in 20 years. I have so many friends there that I need. But I'm an English person, I'm a British person, and I like my roots. I mean I lived in France too for a while, it's good to go and experience as many different countries as you can, that's one of the great things about touring, you see how other people live and you see it for yourself and you see that the propaganda you're fed on television isn't exactly true. That's one of the reasons I love Russia, I love the Russian people very much. When we went there in 1979, I found them very similar in fact, to American people, very kind, very outgoing, very generous people. You would never have believed that, until you went and saw for yourself. So travelling, which is a pain in the arse, by the way, has also broadened my outlook on everything. A lot of my prejudices have gone and my preconceived ideas of people and things have changed by travelling.

Why do you think it was that Bernie, the Lincoln lad, stayed in America, and not you?
EJ Of the two of us it's quite remarkable. It was odds on that if anybody was going to move to America it would have been me with the flamboyant

costumes and the showbiz and things like that, rather than Bernie the farm boy. But that's another example of our relationship being kind of oddball. He loves it there, it suits him, and it suits me to be here.

1976

1974

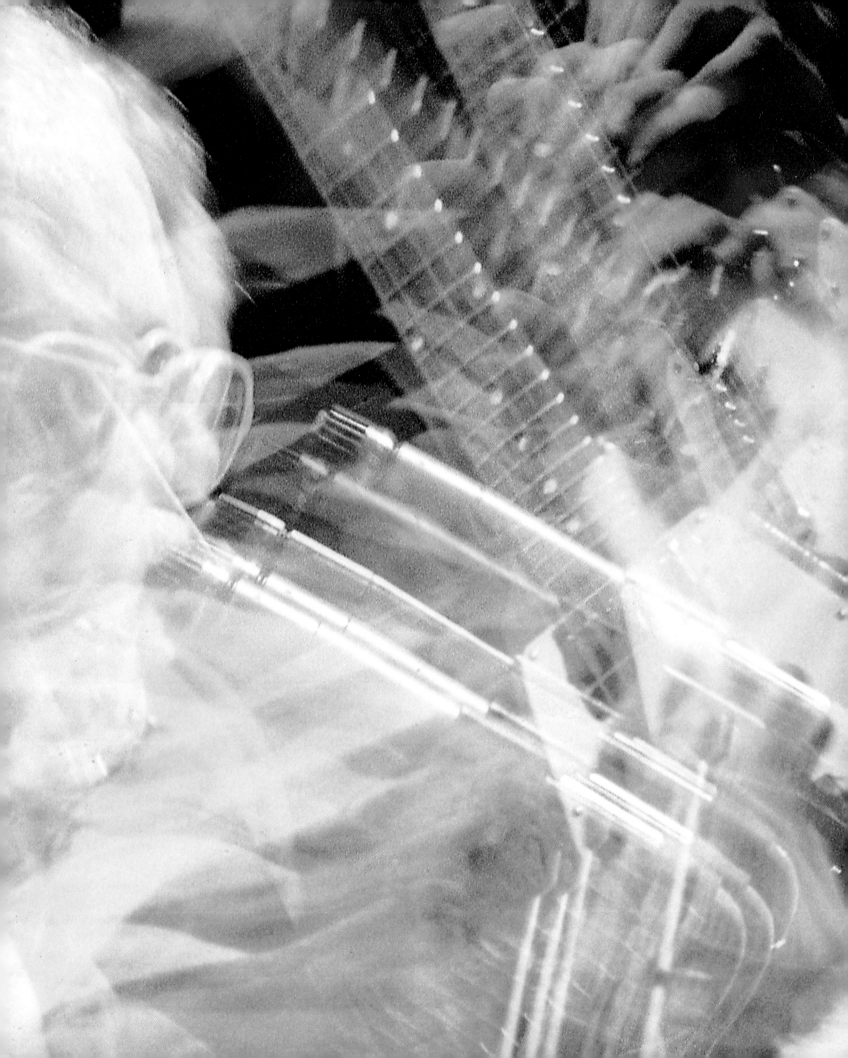

After Blue Moves *why did you feel you needed a break from each other?*

BT After *Blue Moves*, I didn't think we had any choice but to take a break. It was the syndrome of total excess and I mean that on a personal level as well as from the standpoint of fame. There was a time in the mid-seventies when you couldn't sneeze without hearing Elton John's name. It seemed like everything we did was gonna be number one. You can't imagine the pressure. We'd had three albums in a row that went straight into the Billboard charts at number one. *Captain Fantastic* was the first album in history to go straight in at number one, we did it twice after that and nobody's done it since. Sometimes I wish that hadn't happened. We had Elton playing every conceivable stadium. We played Dodger Stadium for two days. There was nowhere else to go and I just felt people must be sick of reading about us. We tried to downplay it, but it made no difference, and it affected us. I had to run away from it because I was frightened to keep going. I was frightened of failure. In this business there's a pinnacle you can reach, but ultimately you've got to sink down. Everybody sinks down. Everybody from The Stones to The Beatles to Springsteen. You've got to drop to that next plateau and stay there, that's where talent ends up. If you don't have that talent, you're a flash in the pan, you just go straight down the toilet. I was afraid of that, so I ran away and I found different ways to escape.

EJ After a while, we both needed a break to write with other people, but there was never any question of us splitting up. I wrote the *Single Man*

album with Gary Osborne, and Bernie had an album out with Alice Cooper, so people put two and two together and said, oh, they've broken up. But it's sometimes necessary to be apart, and he was living in Los Angeles, while I was living in England. That elasticity in our friendship, and the trust to be able to write without getting too *jealous* is important. I think there *were* points when we were both jealous, but we had to give way to that feeling and let it go, because otherwise the relationship would have been too crowded.

You've accused Bernie of writing very sad lyrics, but when you were on your own you went off and wrote Song for Guy?

EJ I love sad songs, I love sad music. I like listening to Handel, I like listening to Elgar, the Enigma Variations, and Nimrod; music that makes me cry, music that would be played at funerals, church music. I'm fascinated with death as far as lyrics and melodies go, hence *Funeral for a Friend*, hence *Song For Guy*, hence *The Man Who Never Died*, which was another instrumental. I just like that sort of music.

He talks about being jealous of the people that you wrote with when you were writing with other people. Did you ever feel that about him?

BT I felt frustrated. Jealousy's such a strange emotion. You either let jealousy flare up or you keep it so deep down that you don't even know it's there and it manifests itself in other forms – you become cynical. So, yeah, I was probably jealous because I thought maybe we could do better together but I knew we couldn't be together at the time.

Had fame affected the relationship between you and Elton?

BT It affected each of us individually, we both had problems with fame but it was never anything to do with us together. Fame never tore us apart and made us fight. It made us fight with ourselves, internally we battled with our own demons and hopefully we've beaten them. We've had times when we've separated. Those times came when I started living here full time and he was living in England. We both had personal problems that caused us to search out different individuals and those different individuals were catalysts to working separately. We did have a time when we worked individually and I don't think either of us created anything particularly great. I had fun and did some okay work and he came out with a couple of things that were worthwhile.

But you did have success during the separation?

BT We both had success in that break-off period, but that period is a lot shorter than people seem to realise. People have this notion that it was years and years. He made one or two complete albums without any input from me, and then it started to slip back in again and we made several albums which I was a part of and I don't think they were particularly great either. On those individual albums we may have written a few songs that were really good – things like *Empty Garden*. But Elton and I don't work well when other people are involved. We really don't, it's all or nothing. The best albums we've made are albums which have been a complete union. When other people have been involved the individual songs may be okay but there isn't that overall feeling of serenity and completeness that encompassed our greatest albums. We're a real united team and I think that's the only way it can work.

British tour 1976

JOHN LENNON

Elton and Lennon, Madison Square Garden 1974

Madison Square Garden 1974

How did you feel recording in the studio with John Lennon?

EJ It was great. He was so easy. When I played on his album *Walls*, I found it very difficult, I had to put my voice onto his and it was very hard. He's got a unique phrasing and it took me a long time to do it. It sounds simple but it was one of the hardest things I've done. But it was still great fun for me to play on the John Lennon album. I mean I played on a Lennon album, I played on a Dylan album, so I'm all right. I've done something with my life.

What was it like, being on stage with him at Madison Square Garden?

EJ It was an unforgettable experience. Grown road managers were crying, there was a ten minute ovation and it sends shivers up and down my spine even to think of it now. Up to that point in my career it was the biggest accolade I'd ever been given by anybody – that he wanted to come on stage with me.

Didn't John Lennon drag you on stage at Madison Square Garden?

BT I didn't have any choice because he threatened to throw up on me if I didn't go on with him. Elton had played on *Whatever Gets You Through the Night* and he'd made this bet with John, because John was hanging out with us at the time, that if *Whatever Gets You Through the Night* got to number one John had to come and play with us on stage, and thank God it was number one and John came on. But there was so much stuff that went on backstage that night because that was the night that he got back with Yoko. It was pretty intense and John was incredibly nervous about performing anyway. He hadn't performed in years. He was used to being buried by the band and sinking into the background. Believe it or not I think Yoko took a lot of that sort of pressure off him, you know he felt that he wasn't the only one up there. So when he had to go on and do it on his own, he was so petrified that he said I'm gonna throw up if you don't come up with me. So I went on with him and I said to him you're on your own now. And he was unbelievable, that was probably one of the best shows we've ever, ever done. The emotion generated in that building that night, you'll never see again.

Did he ever give you advice?

EJ The only advice he ever gave me was to enjoy my career as much as I could, and I was enjoying it at that point. He was very kind and he was very considerate not only to me but to other people in the room who he didn't know. He was not one of those people who come in and just home in on me and ignore everybody else. He had the good manners to involve everybody and be nice to everybody. I mean he went with my band to the airport, he took my mother and father out to dinner in New York.

What impressed you most about him?

BT His honesty. I spent a lot of time with him, he was the only person that I ever met who I absolutely idolised, but when I was with him I didn't feel that I was with somebody that I idolised. He always made you feel comfortable and he taught you things without you even knowing you were being taught. He taught me a lot about writing and humility. I always felt that if you could be John Lennon and have that much humility it just brought everything back down to earth.

What were you doing when you heard about his death?

EJ I landed in Melbourne in Australia and my manager came onto the plane and told me that he'd been killed and I just didn't believe it. It didn't sink in for a long time. When I see an image of him I miss him a great deal. When I say I miss him it would be totally false of me to sit here and say that we were bosom buddies. We did have a period when we hung out together and it was wonderful – you don't have to see them all the time to be someone's friend. He was special and everybody knows it.

BT I was at my house in Los Angeles. My wife and I were supposed to be going out for dinner when a friend of mine called me up just before we were leaving and told me. The initial shock of anybody's death that is close to you is not as bad as the shock that comes later so you tend to be able to deal with it relatively well up front. But I couldn't go out, because I knew that if I went out that's all I was gonna hear. I went into my office and I closed the door and I stayed there for a day. I wouldn't watch the news and I wouldn't read a paper because I didn't want to hear about it. That was when I wrote *Empty Garden*, I knew in the back of my mind that everybody would be doing the same thing and I remember thinking to myself, God, is this me cashing in, am I being cold, am I being calculating? But I suddenly realised it was the only thing I could do. I couldn't cry because that comes later, and it was the only way that I

Elton and Lennon, Madison Square Garden 1974

could express myself and the thing is I really don't remember what I wrote. I just wrote it and it didn't surface till much later on. I felt numb for days. Losing John was like the world losing a limb.

How did you and Bernie write Empty Garden*?*

EJ Well I wrote *The Man Who Never Died* which is an instrumental for John. But Bernie came up with a lyric that I thought was really special. Initially I didn't want to put anything down with a lyric on it because I thought it would sound corny, but I wanted to do something. I wanted to put something on tape that would show that I loved the man and I was able to put an instrumental down and a song. Whenever I hear either of them I get moved because it brings back memories of someone who was very, very special to me. I've performed *Empty Garden* once on tour, but I won't do it again because I find it very hard to sing – it upsets me.

Did you support Bernie through his difficult times?

EJ I think so. But I don't think we really had that many difficult times when we were younger, I think the difficult things started when we became successful; when relationships started with other people and we had money and fame. It was never a problem when we weren't famous, it was lovely, it was very innocent.

Are you best friends?

EJ Yeah. No question. We don't see a lot of each other now because I live here and he lives there, but I feel very much that we're closer now than we've ever been, and I can't ever see us not writing together.

Do you tell each other everything?

EJ We tell each other nothing. That's the problem. We know what's going on in each other's lives but it's very hard to crack us. We've never communicated really on a personal level, it's been an emotional relationship. It's very hard to describe but there are things about Bernie I still don't know and stuff he still doesn't know about me.

You and Elton have been through many ups and downs. Do you think of each other as emotional supports?

BT Elton and I are a lot of things to each other. I don't know if we're emotional supports because we don't spend enough time around each other. I think we know each other far more than we give ourselves credit for, but emotional supports tend to be physically there at the time you need them. It's not necessarily something you can find on the end of a phone and Elton and I are constantly on the end of a phone. But I don't think we can deal with each other's emotions because I think we come from different points. I don't think he can deal with my problems and I don't think I can deal with his, but I know that he's always there for my support and I'm always there for his support, and I think that's enough.

> "The evidence, from the last album shows Elton and Bernie growing old gracefully. They're still great rockers but it's a little simpler now. I've got a feeling that Elton isn't quite so flamboyant, and he's probably gonna calm down as the years go by, and that's great, because the music will reflect that, too. It will become a little more serene perhaps."
>
> *Eric Clapton*

You've talked a lot about Bernie's good qualities, does he have any bad ones?

EJ Stubborness is Bernie's worst quality. He's very hard to get into. He's very shut down, very emotionally shut down. I don't know if I know the real Bernie and I don't think he does either you know. I'm just getting to know the real me. But trying to find out who you really are is hard. Bernie's very hard to get to know, he's lovely, he's loveable and everything but there is a certain loneliness about him. I think that there was a certain loneliness about me too. Maybe it brought us together but we've always been loners, we are both very much our own people.

How do you think he would describe you?

EJ Infuriating might be one of the words. Infuriating, kind, mad, exasperating.

What frustrates you about Elton?

BT As stubborn as I am, I think he's equally stubborn and maybe that's a good point between the two of us. Elton has come to terms with a lot of demons in his life and I think he's probably changed himself in a lot of ways. He's notorious for his mood swings. He can be Santa Claus one minute, he can be the devil incarnate the next, but hell, that makes him interesting. I've damned him to all eternity at certain points, and I'm sure he's done the same to me because I've been equally guilty of being a jerk. He's frustrated me and annoyed me to the point where I've just said to hell with this, I can't deal with you anymore. There have been times on tours where he's been a total arsehole and I've said that's it, I'm out of here, I'm gone. But after 25 years, if two people as close as he and I are don't get up each other's nose occasionally then that's not healthy. Opposites attract, and that's what's kept this union solid for the last 25 years. It's chalk and cheese, it's fire and ice. He's my best friend, he's my worst enemy. I love the guy to death, I can't say any more.

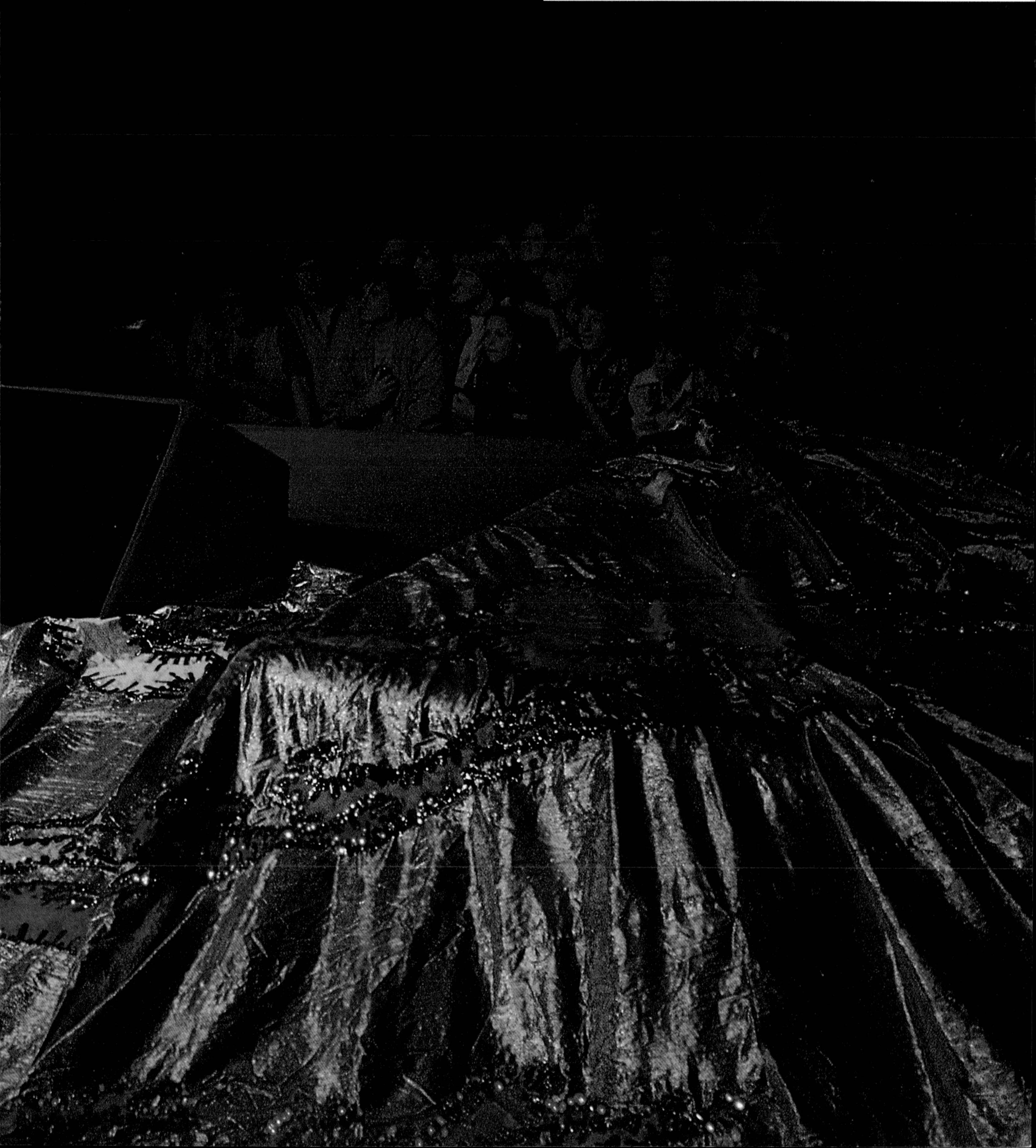

Do you believe in fate?

EJ I believe totally in fate. I think you have to take risks to get what you want. If I hadn't taken the risk to leave Bluesology, this wouldn't ever have happened. That was a courageous decision for a tubby young organ player who had nothing else to offer. You have to keep that element of risk going throughout your career otherwise you won't last. I still want to compete with the youngsters and the other song writers. I'm still in search of the perfect song. To have ambitions is so important if you don't want to grow tired of what you do. There are times in my career where I've grown tired of what I've done and it's shown in my stage work and it's shown in my recording work but I don't feel like that now. I've been doing this for over twenty years and there's been a lot of albums and a lot of songs and I'm not fed up, so I'm lucky.

BT If anything is destined it was for him and I to be together. Some higher power said let's put these two together and irritate the world. If we give anybody any pleasure, if we give one in ten pleasure, it's a great feeling. I don't take compliments very well, but I never get tired, of people on the street complimenting us. And when they stop talking, I'm gonna start looking for them.

What if you hadn't met Bernie?

EJ There's no point in even projecting like that. What has happened has been miraculous, it's been exciting, it's been enthralling, it's been beyond your wildest dreams, it's been sad, it's been tough, it's been hard and it's been easy. I'm just coming to terms with my life, trying to take stock of who I am, what's happened to me and trying to change the way I live and appreciate the things I have more, and that's taken me twenty years to get to. This business can create monsters out of you and we've both been monsters in our own right, the way we've behaved and so on. We're both from simple backgrounds and what has happened to us is quite breathtaking. I really do like life but there have been times in my career when I haven't and I didn't want to go on but now I do want to go on and having Bernie in my life is such an important thing.

At 26 you said "Our best is yet to come." You'd already written two classics then; Your Song *and* Daniel. *Do you still feel that?*

EJ Yeah absolutely. I don't dwell on the past, I mean I never listen to our old albums, I hear them on the radio. I mean one has to sing a certain percentage of your songs on stage to please people and if you want to end up in Las Vegas that's fine. I could stop now and go and put on my glittery suit again and my glittery glasses and my high heeled shoes and sing there for the rest of my life and earn a million dollars a week. But, I don't want to do that. I never wanted to do that. I just wanted to write things that mean something to me and hopefully to other people – that is a wonderful thing to do.

How do you feel about the tribute album?

EJ The tribute album's something that I haven't really had much to do with and it's good that I haven't, because I get embarrassed. I'm so flattered by the people that are doing it. It's wonderful to be respected by one's peers and the people that are doing this album are good people, good friends and great musicians.

BT The fact that people are doing the tribute album is very overwhelming for me. There are people on this album that I idolised before I even knew I wanted to write songs and that's a humbling experience. It's wonderful.

Do you see your future together?
BT Oh, definitely. It's hard to imagine a future without him. We've got a lot to do.

How would you describe your relationship with Elton?
BT My relationship with Elton is intense, without being intense. There's a respect there which didn't surface for a long time. We started out as childish buddies, and we enjoyed each other's company and there was brotherly love there. It emerged into something more and something that I think neither of us have come to terms with. If I remain anything with Elton it's a real fan. It's a great honour to be able to work with somebody who is such a brilliant musician and singer.

Is there any one song that you would say sums up your relationship with Elton?
BT The one that comes to mind is *Two Rooms at the End of the World* which was a song written purely about us, about the differences between us. It's a

song saying, you can judge us individually but together this is what we do, accept it or get out of here.

Do you have any favourite lyrics that stay with you or lyrics that describe the two of you?
EJ *We All Fall in Love Sometimes* is very personal to me because it sums up the love that we did have together and that we still do. When we met it was like two children getting together and being brothers and that was very special. I would have to say that that means more to me than anything else we've written.

He said We All Fall in Love Sometimes *was the song that he would choose to sum up your relationship. Are you surprised by that?*
BT No I don't think that's strange at all. The *Captain Fantastic* album is our homage to ourselves. It's all about us. *Captain Fantastic and the Brown Dirt Cowboy* is totally about us, about me and him. It's country boy, city boy, town mouse, country mouse. *We All Fall in Love Sometimes* is a very personal song because it's the finale. The album is a story about two people with an intensity to write and the only way they can achieve that is by being together. That album's about learning to write, it's about learning to survive – it's about the

time when the only thing we had was each other, and a couple of other people that were behind us. That album is about working on the *Empty Sky* album with Steve Brown. After those sessions Elton and I and Steve would go into Oxford Street to the Wimpy bar, there was nothing grand about it. It is about trying to write the best song possible and the last song *We All Fall in Love*

Sometimes is about having achieved that. We've done it, we've created our first child and now we're allowed to go our separate ways. We'll always have that child, that child's always gonna be in our lives but you and I are allowed to go away separately now. We'll keep on doing it but now we can do it and be apart from each other.

D I S C O G R A P H Y

UK ALBUMS

Jun	1969	Empty Sky
Mar	1970	Elton John
Oct	1970	Tumbleweed Connection
Apr	1971	17.11.70 (Live)
Apr	1971	Friends
Nov	1971	Madman Across The Water
May	1972	Honky Chateau
Jan	1973	Don't Shoot Me I'm The Piano Player
Oct	1973	Goodbye Yellow Brick Road
Jun	1974	Caribou
Nov	1974	Greatest Hits Vol. 1
May	1975	Captain Fantastic And The Brown Dirt Cowboy
Oct	1975	Rock Of The Westies
Apr	1976	Here And There (Live)
Oct	1976	Blue Moves
Sep	1977	Greatest Hits Vol. 2
Oct	1978	A Single Man
Oct	1979	Victim Of Love
May	1980	21 At 33
	1980	The Very Best Of Elton John
May	1981	The Fox
Apr	1982	Jump Up
Oct	1982	Love Songs
Jun	1983	Too Low For Zero
Jun	1984	Breaking Hearts
Nov	1985	Ice On Fire
Nov	1986	Leather Jackets
Sep	1987	Live In Australia
Jul	1988	Reg Strikes Back
Sep	1989	Sleeping With The Past
Sep	1990	The Very Best Of Elton John

UK SINGLES

Jul	1965	Come Back Baby/Times Getting Tougher Than Tough (Bluesology)
Feb	1966	Mr Frantic/Everyday (I Have The Blues) (Bluesology)
Oct	1967	Since I Found You Baby/Just A Little Bit (Bluesology)
Mar	1968	I've Been Loving You/Here's To The Next Time
Jan	1969	Lady Samantha/All Across The Havens
May	1969	It's Me That You Need/Just Like Strange Rain
Mar	1970	Border Song/Bad Side Of The Moon
Jun	1970	Rock And Roll Madonna/Grey Seal
Jan	1971	Your Song/Into The Old Man's Shoes
Apr	1971	Friends/Honey Roll
Apr	1972	Rocket Man/Holiday Inn/Goodbye
Aug	1972	Honky Cat/Lady Samantha/It's Me That You Need
Oct	1972	Crocodile Rock/Elderberry Wine
Jan	1973	Daniel/Skyline Pigeon
Jun	1973	Saturday Night's Alright For Fighting/Jack Rabbit/Whenever You're Ready (We'll Go Steady Again)
Sep	1973	Goodbye Yellow Brick Road/Screw You
Nov	1973	Step Into Christmas/Ho! Ho! Ho! (Who'd Be A Turkey At Christmas)
Feb	1974	Candle In The Wind/Bennie And The Jets
May	1974	Don't Let The Sun Go Down On Me/Sick City
Aug	1974	The Bitch Is Back/Cold Highway
Nov	1974	Lucy In The Sky With Diamonds/One Day At A Time
Feb	1975	Philadelphia Freedom/I Saw Her Standing There
May	1975	Someone Saved My Life Tonight/House Of Cards
Sep	1975	Island Girl/Sugar On The Floor
Jan	1976	Grow Some Funk Of Your Own/I Feel Like A Bullet (In The Gun Of Robert Ford)
Mar	1976	Pinball Wizard/Harmony
Jun	1976	Don't Go Breaking My Heart/Snow Queen
Sep	1976	Bennie & The Jets/Rock & Roll Madonna
Oct	1976	Sorry Seems To Be The Hardest Word/Shoulder Holster
Feb	1977	Crazy Water/Chameleon
Apr	1977	The Goldigger Song/Jimmy, Brian, Elton, Eric
May	1977	Four From Four Eyes EP: Your Song/Rocket Man/Saturday Night's Alright For Fighting/Whenever You're Ready (We'll Go Steady Again)
Jun	1977	Bite Your Lip (Get Up And Dance)/Chicago
Mar	1978	Ego/Flintstone Boy
Sep	1978	Funeral For A Friend: Loves Lies Bleeding/We All Fall In Love Sometimes/Curtains
Sep	1978	Lady Samantha/Skyline Pigeon
Sep	1978	Your Song/Border Song
Sep	1978	Honky Cat/Sixty Years On
Sep	1978	Country Comfort/Crocodile Rock
Sep	1978	Rocket Man/Daniel
Sep	1978	Sweet Painted Lady/Goodbye Yellow Brick Road
Sep	1978	Philadelphia Freedom/Lucy In The Sky With Diamonds
Sep	1978	Candle In The Wind/I Feel Like A Bullet (In The Gun Of Robert Ford)
Sep	1978	Don't Let The Sun Go Down On Me/Someone Saved My Life Tonight
Sep	1978	The Bitch Is Back/Grow Some Funk Of Your Own
Sep	1978	Island Girl/Saturday Night's Alright For Fighting
Sep	1978	Pinball Wizard/Benny & The Jets
Oct	1978	Part Time Love/Cry At Night
Nov	1978	Song For Guy/Lovesick
Apr	1979	Are You Ready For Love (two parts)
Apr	1979	Are You Ready For Love/Three Way Love Affair/Mama Can't Buy Love
Sep	1979	Victim Of Love/Strangers
Dec	1979	Johnny B Goode/Thunder In The Night
May	1980	Little Jeannie/Conquer The Sun/Johnny B Goode (extended)/Thunder in the Night – 12"
Aug	1980	Sartorial Eloquence/White Man Danger/Cartier
Nov	1980	Harmony/Mona Lisas And Mad Hatters
Nov	1980	Dear God/Tactics
Nov	1980	Dear God/Tactics/Steal Away Child/Love So Cold (double single)
Mar	1981	I Saw Her Standing There/Whatever Gets You Through The Night/Lucy In The Sky With Diamonds

May	1981	Nobody Wins/Fools In Fashion
Jul	1981	Just Like Belgium/Can't Get Over Getting Over Losing You
Nov	1981	Loving You Is Sweeter Than Ever/24 Hours
Mar	1982	Blue Eyes/Hey Papa Legba
May	1982	Empty Garden/Take Me Down To The Ocean
Sep	1982	Princess/The Retreat
Nov	1982	All Quiet On The Western Front/Where Have All The Good Times Gone
Apr	1983	I Guess That's Why They Call It The Blues/Lord Choc Ice Goes Mental
Jul	1983	I'm Still Standing/Earn While You Learn
Jul	1983	I'm Still Standing (Remix)/Earn While You Learn 12″
Oct	1983	Kiss The Bride/Dreamboat
Oct	1983	Kiss The Bride/Dreamboat/Ego/Song For Guy
Nov	1983	Cold As Christmas/Crystal
Dec	1983	Cold As Christmas/Crystal/Don't Go Breaking My Heart/Snow Queen (double single)
May	1984	Sad Songs (Say So Much)/Simple Man
Aug	1984	Passengers/Lonely Boy
Oct	1984	Who Wears These Shoes/Tortured
Oct	1984	Who Wears These Shoes/Tortured/I Heard It Through The Grapevine (Live) – 12″
Feb	1985	Breaking Hearts (Ain't What It Used To Be)/In Neon
Jun	1985	Act Of War parts 1 & 2 (with Millie Jackson)
Jun	1985	Act Of War parts 1 to 4 (with Millie Jackson) – 12″
Jun	1985	Act Of War – remixes – 12″
Sep	1985	Nikita/The Man Who Never Died/Sorry Seems To Be The Hardest Word (Live)/I'm Still Standing (Live) (double single)
Nov	1985	Wrap Her Up/Restless (Live)
Nov	1985	Wrap Her Up (extended)/Restless (live) Nikita/Cold As Chritmas (double 12″)
Nov	1985	That's What Friends Are For (Dionne Warwick And Friends – Elton John, Stevie Wonder and Gladys Knight)/reverse by Dionne Warwick
Nov	1985	That's What Friends Are For/plus instrumental version and reverse by Dionne Warwick – 12″
Feb	1986	Cry To Heaven/Candy By The Pound
Feb	1986	Cry To Heaven/Candy By The Pound/Rock n Roll Medley 12″
Feb	1986	Cry To Heaven/Candy By The Pound/Rock n Roll Medley/Your Song (double single)
Sep	1986	Heartache All Over The World/Highlander
Sep	1986	Heartache All Over The World/Highlander/Heartache All Over the World (7″ version) – 12″
Sep	1986	Heartache All Over The World/Highlander/Nikita/Passengers/I'm Still Standing (cassette)
Nov	1986	Slow Rivers/Billy And The Kids
Nov	1986	Slow Rivers/Billy And The Kids/Lord Of The Flies – 12″
Dec	1986	Slow Rivers/Billy And The Kids/Nikita/Blue Eyes/I Guess That's Why They Call It The Blues (cassette)
Jun	1987	Your Song (live)/Don't Let The Sun Go Down On Me (live)
Jun	1987	Your Song (live)/Don't Let The Sun Go Down On Me (live)/The Greatest Discovery (live)/I Need You To Turn To (live) – 12″
Dec	1987	Candle In The Wind (live)/Sorry Seems To Be The Hardest Word (live)
Dec	1987	Candle In The Wind (live)/Sorry Seems To Be The Hardest Word (live)/Your Song (live)/Don't Let The Sun Go Down On Me (live) – 12″
May	1988	Candle In The Wind/I Guess That's Why They Call It The Blues/I'm Still Standing/Nikita (video)
May	1988	I Don't Wanna Go On With You Like That/Rope Around A Fool
May	1988	I Don't Wanna Go On With You Like That/I Don't Wanna Go On With You Like That (7″ version)/Rope Around A Fool – 12″
May	1988	I Don't Wanna Go On With You Like That/Rope Around A Fool/I Don't Wanna Go On With You Like That (remix) CD
Jun	1988	I Don't Wanna Go On With You Like That/Rope Around A Fool/Interview
Aug	1988	Town Of Plenty/Whipping Boy
Aug	1988	Town Of Plenty/Whipping Boy/My Baby's A Saint – 12″
Nov	1988	A Word In Spanish/Heavy Traffic
Nov	1988	A Word In Spanish/Heavy Traffic/Medley (live in Australia) – 12″
Nov	1988	A Word In Spanish/Heavy Traffic/Medley (live in Australia)/Daniel – CD
Jul	1989	Healing Hand/Dancing In The End Zone
Jul	1989	Healing Hands (extended remix)/Healing Hands (7″ version)/Dancing In The End Zone – 12″
Jul	1989	Healing Hands/Sad Songs (Say So Much) (Live)/Dancing In The End Zone – CD
Oct	1989	Sacrifice/Love Is A Cannibal
Oct	1989	Sacrifice/Love Is A Cannibal/Durban Deep – 12″
Jun	1990	Sacrifice/Healing Hands
Jun	1990	Sacrifice/Healing Hands/Durban Deep – 12″
Aug	1990	Club At The End Of The Street/Whispers
Aug	1990	Club At The End Of The Street/Whispers/I Don't Wanna Go On With You Like That – 12″
Oct	1990	You Gotta Love Someone/Medicine Man
Oct	1990	You Gotta Love Someone/Medicine Man/Medicine Man (Adamski version) – 12″
Nov	1990	Easier To Walk Away/I Swear I Heard The Night Talking
Nov	1990	Easier To Walk Away/I Swear I Heard The Night Talking/Made For Me – 12″
Feb	1991	Don't Let The Sun Go Down On Me/Song For Guy
Feb	1991	Don't Let The Sun Go Down On Me/Song For Guy/Sorry Seems To Be The Hardest Word – 12″

We All Fall In Love Sometimes

Wise men say
It looks like rain today.
It crackled on the speakers
And trickled down the sleepy subway trains.
For heavy eyes could hardly hold us,
Aching legs that often told us
It's all worth it
We all fall in love sometimes.

The full moon's bright
And starlight filled the evening.
We wrote it and I played it,
Something happened it's so strange this feeling.
Naive notions that were childish
Simple tunes that try to hide it,
But when it comes
We all fall in love sometimes.

Did we, didn't we, should we couldn't we
I'm not sure 'cause sometimes we're so blind.
Struggling through the day
When even your best friend says,
Don't you find
We all fall in love sometimes.

And only passing time
Could kill the boredom we acquired
Running with the loosers for awhile.
But our Empty Sky was filled with laughter
Just before the flood,
Painting worried faces with a smile.

ACKNOWLEDGEMENTS:

Thanks To:

Alan Finch
Barry Plummer
Barrie Wentzell
Bob Alford
Bob Carlos Clarke
Bob Gruen (Starfile Inc)
Bryan Forbes
David Nutter
Denis O'Regan
Ed Caraeff
George Wilkes
Gered Mankowitz
Herb Ritts
H. Goodwin
Juergen Teller
Michael Childers
Michael Putland (London Features)
Peter Vernon
Phillip Ollerenshaw
Randee St. Nicholas
Ron Pownall
Sam Emerson
Terry O'Neill

Photographs from The John Reid Enterprises
Archive and Private Collections